RUNNING SCARED

Fiona Brennan

Introduction

This story alternates between Manchester and Rowan, a fictional village in Wales.

Luke lives in Manchester and is a persistent truant and shoplifter. His stepdad is demanding he steals more cigarettes and he's trying not to make any more personal appearances at the Magistrates Court.

Following a violent encounter Luke is trying to avoid the local gang, the Ardwick Barmy Army (ABA).

Spud is the leader of the ABA and he's out for blood as his massive tribute to MUFC keeps being defaced by a rival with blue paint and changing to MCFC.

In Rowan local thug Tommo is selling drugs for someone from Manchester as part of a County Lines operation and may even be growing his own.

Chapter 1 – In the City – Late for School

In a small, cold flat in Ardwick, Manchester:
Luke was fumbling with his 'phone to switch off the alarm when his stepdad, Damian barged into his bedroom. Damian leaned over him and muttered, 'I need more cigs, make sure you get plenty this time.'

Trying not to breathe too deeply as Damian always smelt as if he'd brushed his teeth with cheap whisky, Luke said, 'they've got cameras and stuff now at Zach's. I can't get away with anything from there.'

'Well get them from somewhere else,' Damian said.

'Why don't you just go and buy some?'

'Because I'm skint. I lost some money last night.'

Probably in a poker game, thought Luke. As Damian trapped Luke with his skinny arms, Luke noticed the ginger hairs covering several tattoos which had recently been touched up. He had a roulette wheel, spinning dice and playing cards on one arm and a sleeve on the other of the devil riding a motorbike. He also had three sixes just behind his left ear, which looked like an ugly spider and made Luke's skin crawl. It was easily visible as he shaved his hair into a short crew cut, which he was convinced hid his imminent baldness.

Damian wasn't the worst parent Luke had ever had, but he was in the top two. First place was still held by Luke's real dad, who was doing a stretch in Strangeways for robbing a betting shop. Luke didn't know what he wanted to do with his life, but he didn't want to end up like either of those two losers. He knew if he didn't get some cigs Damian would be twitchy and irritable. He was already obnoxious; he didn't want to add grouchy to the list.

He pushed passed Damian and went to the dingy bathroom. Stepping over Damian's discarded boxers, Luke had a quick shower. He got dressed in most of his school uniform - he couldn't remember the last time he wore his tie or blazer. Then applied gel to his dirty-blond hair and spent ages pushing and pulling it into shape, making sure it looked as if he hadn't spent any time on it. Glancing in the mirror he was finally satisfied with the result.

Entering the cramped kitchen, he noticed the distinct smell of burnt toast, which meant his mum was running late again. She dropped a few pound coins onto the table for his lunch and threw a couple of Damian's empty lager cans in the recycling bin.

'Can you lend me a few quid, Beth?' Wheedled Damian.

'You only got paid a couple of days ago. What have you done with your money?' Luke's mum wanted to know.

'I've bought something for you if you must know. It's for your birthday,' he lied, winking at Luke over her shoulder.

'Oh, you shouldn't have.' She searched through her purse. 'I can only spare a tenner,' she said handing it over to him. Luke assumed Damian must owe money to someone and a tenner probably wasn't likely to make

4

much difference to Damian, but his mum might have to skip lunch.

Then addressing Luke, Beth said, 'get to school on time and don't go getting into trouble with Robbie,' picking fluff off his shoulder. She touched his cheek and then dashed out, pulling the door closed behind her. So, no chance of having a quick word with her about Damian, he thought. Not that she'd listen anyway.

He went back to his bedroom to grab his school bag and Damian came up behind him, making him jump. He was forever slithering around the place.

'Try and get a drop of the good stuff, as well,' demanded Damian.

'Mum will kill me if I get in trouble again.'

'So don't get caught. It'll probably be easier if you go to one of the shops in the precinct at lunchtime when they're busy,' said Damian, stuffing his keys and a nearly empty fag packet in his leather jacket. That must be what passes for parental advice in his world, thought Luke.

He grabbed his hoody, picked up his keys and left the flat by the back exit. The wall along the alley was covered in a tribute to Manchester United. It had started as an enormous outline of the initials MUFC in the team colours of red, white and black, and had been added to over the years. The outside of the doors to the flats had been painted like a turnstile with two new players who had recently signed for the club entering the ground.

The main tag on the work was from Spud, the hard-line leader of the Ardwick Barmy Army. He and Luke

5

despised each other as a result of several encounters over the previous couple of years. On one occasion Luke had taken a shortcut through a nearby graveyard and stumbled across Spud, who beat him up so badly he could hardly eat or walk for a week. The police had been involved and Spud had been charged with assault and ordered to attend a Youth Rehabilitation Centre for several weekends. The offence occurred the week before Spud's sixteenth birthday, so he avoided a harsher sentence. He'd been doing a drug deal amongst the dead after dark but told the judge he was visiting his grandad's grave as he didn't want anyone to see him upset. Spud respected neither the living nor the dead, but the gullible judge gave him the benefit of the doubt.

The street art had been vandalised a few times recently. Someone who was either mad or brave had started adding comments slagging off specific United players. Spud had accused practically everyone who passed by of damaging it and had beaten up several kids who he suspected of being the rival artist, resulting in one of them needing extensive dental surgery. There had been a turf war going on for a while as a result.

Luke dawdled down the road and noticing an empty beer can he absent-mindedly kicked it along the pavement. The grey lump of his school was in the distance, just past the local pub, The Old Crow. It was very popular locally as somewhere you could hand a shopping list of items to one of the barmen and collect them a few days later, with no questions asked and a very reasonable price tag. No one was quite sure who lifted the goods, but they were efficient. He was about to kick the can again when he noticed the back of Spud's head further up the road. It was easily recognisable as he had a prominent scar across the back of his skull and acne scars across his face and neck. He was with a couple of the members of his gang, the Ardwick Barmy Army, including his gorgeous girlfriend, Natasha. Luke had never been able to understand why she was with Spud; she had always seemed funny and bright when she was in the same lessons. Unfortunately, she hadn't been to school for months.

He could see Chucky with his distinctive red hair and Travis with his afro punching each other on the arm to see who would stop first. Their gang was truly an equal-opportunity employer. They had work for everyone, regardless of age, race, religion or gender. And everyone was guaranteed to be treated equally badly; there was very little opportunity for advancement, they had to work unsociable hours, there was zero pension even if you lived long enough to claim it, no job security, and no one to complain to if you were unhappy with the terms and conditions. They were all dressed in their trademark black tracksuits, so Luke left the can where it was and took the next left and left again back to the flat. As he went, he kept glancing over his shoulder to make sure the ABA wasn't coming after him. Luke had refused to join their gang, and if you weren't with them, you were against them.

'Damn,' he thought to himself 'why did they have to be up this early?' He had intended to go to school today, which was quite unusual for a Monday.

He hated school, the only days he enjoyed were Tuesdays and Fridays, and that was purely for his PE lessons. The PE teacher was Mr Strachan, and Luke still remembered cringing at his parents' evening when Mr Strachan had praised him to his mum and said that he could have a bright future ahead of him if he would just apply himself and go to college. Later his mum had said, 'Go to college? He's got to be kidding, that would be at least two years wasted when you could start work straight away. If you couldn't get something you prefer you could get a job at my place; they've started offering apprenticeships at the sausage factory.'

'That's because it smells disgusting, it's boring, and the pay is crap.'

'It's better than minimum wage, and the forklift truck drivers earn even more.'

Luke had dropped the conversation. He knew his mum meant well but he would hate to work at the sausage factory. Unfortunately, he couldn't imagine any job that would use his skills on a running track. He loved cross-country running, it left him physically exhausted but mentally revived, but he needed to think of a way to put his talent to use in a way that would earn him money.

Luke had watched the London Marathon on television and noticed that a lot of the runners had travelled from all over the world to participate. Several of the runners had given up their jobs and just ran for a living. He thought it

8

would be great if it was possible to get paid for running through sponsorship or prize money. But he would have to keep it secret from his mates; he didn't have anyone close enough who he could confide in, no one who would understand why he liked running. The ones who bothered to do any activity at all either did boxing or football which was regarded as more acceptable than running for its own sake. He wasn't sure if he would ever be fit enough to do a full marathon but had watched the runners taking part in the half-marathon that took place annually in Manchester.

He was restless and bored as he wandered down the backstreets. He hated having to dodge the ABA and perpetually keep his head down. Eventually, he convinced himself that he should go for a run. He decided that since cross-country runs at school took nearly the whole lesson he would go and run at a decent pace for an hour. Watching the marathon, it didn't look too difficult. The winner was able to hold a conversation within a couple of minutes of completing the course, and he was an old man from somewhere in Africa.

He let himself into his flat and dug out his tracksuit. He quickly changed, grabbed his keys and 'phone and walked down the road away from where his mate Robbie lived, and the ABA. As soon as he was sure he wouldn't be spotted by anyone who knew him, he started running. It felt great to stretch his legs, but he had to keep stopping because of the constant stream of cars and buses. It must feel great when they close the streets for road races, he thought to himself.

It felt good to run without interruption along Ardwick Green Park with its monument to commemorate the dead of the Eighth Ardwicks. He ran along Downing Street and as he passed underneath the Mancunian Way, he could feel the thundering traffic overhead. He went along the appropriately named Dark Lane and kept going until he reached Alan Turing Way, before heading back home along Ashton Old Road.

Stopping to check his 'phone he was staggered to discover he had only been running for thirty minutes. He didn't feel this exhausted after a PE lesson, so he assumed he'd been running faster than usual as he didn't have the whole class to slow him down. He was thirsty and as soon as he found a corner shop, he bought a bottle of juice.

The cool drink revived him, so he ran on for another couple of miles then paused for a couple of minutes to catch his breath. I'd better start running back as I still have to thieve some cigs for Damian, irritated as the thought disturbed his run. Nearing home, he decided he didn't have the energy to go the long way around, so decided to run past Robbie's block of flats. Luke hoped he would be in school for a change - he regularly blamed his asthma for his lack of attendance.

As he ran past Robbie's flat, he spotted the ABA loitering near the recycling bins. They were on the opposite side of the road, but he noticed them quickly stubbing out their cigarettes and running after him. They often chased him because he 'disrespected' them. Luckily, there was plenty of traffic, which slowed them down. However, the traffic didn't hold them up for long, and he saw their reflections in the windows as they gained on him.

Chapter 2 - In the Village – Late for School

Joey and his older brother James were joking with each other as they stuffed toast in their mouths in the large farmhouse kitchen. The farm had been in their family for several generations, but their dad, Paul, had struggled to make a living when most of his herd had contracted bovine TB and had to be culled. He had sold his fields to the Council and now worked as an electrician, a job which frequently took him into Manchester which was 50 miles away from Rowan. The lads were barely paying attention to the radio when they overheard an interview between the DJ and the local councillor.

'So why do the Council want to build these houses?' the DJ asked.

'Because this is a sad little village, and it needs an injection of new life,' replied Reg.

'WHAT? Sad?' The DJ said.

'Sorry, that was the wrong word, I meant sleepy!' Said Reg.

'Well folks, now you know what Reg thinks of Rowan. If you'd like to take part in this discussion, call the show and let me know what you think. Or come to the meeting tonight to have a say.'

Joey laughed as he heard Reg trying to backtrack, but the DJ closed his mic and started playing some music.

'I can't wait for the meeting, an argument or a fight would be the most exciting thing that's happened in a while. Maybe I'll finally have something interesting enough to post on Instagram,' said Joey.

'You won't be able to video the meeting,' said James.

'Oh, shame. Well, should we still go?'

'Yeah, we want to know what the plans are. They might affect us and could be right on our doorstep. See you later,' James said, pulling his jacket on.

Joey threw their plates in the sink, stuffed his sandwiches in his school bag and put his coat on. He quickly glanced in the mirror, smoothed his hair a bit and wiped some butter off his chin. His school was in the next village, as there weren't enough pupils to justify a school in each. He'd missed the bus, so he would have to run to school, which was a fairly common occurrence and allowed him to save his bus fare and train for the run at the same time.

It was the beginning of spring, and he could see his breath in front of him as he climbed over a dry-stone wall, and then dodged between the sheep and the muddy patches. There was a stream at the bottom of the field which he crossed by using the steppingstones that James and he had put there a few years before. It saved them from walking all the way back up the hill to a small bridge.

He was about to climb over a gate into the next field when he saw Tommo's distinct red hair. He was a local lad who had left school a year earlier but had struggled to find a job. Tommo used to play rugby for the village but hadn't attended training for months. The only interaction Joey got from him was pictures he posted on Snapchat of

13

weird images such as a skunk (heroin), a can of coke (cocaine), a dandelion (weed), a diamond (crystal meth), or a KitKat (ketamine) which were the drugs he had available, another reason for Joey to try to avoid him. As he was looking around and weighing up his options Tommo whistled to him. As he approached, Tommo riffled through his pockets. He held out some little plastic bags. Joey stuck his hands in his pockets.

'Here, take them,' said Tommo.

'No, thanks,' said Joey.

'You can have them, for FREE.'

Joey had heard one of the boys at school saying his sister had been given free drugs but was then forced to sell for the gang.

'I don't want them.'

'Well give them to James.'

'He doesn't do drugs.'

'Oh, I forgot, he's a superstar athlete now, isn't he?' He sneered. 'Well, what about your mates at school?'

'None of them do drugs.'

'Yes, they do.'

'How do you know?'

'They're my customers.'

'Well then, give them the free samples when you see them.'

'I don't want to give existing users freebies.'

'I'm not being caught with your stuff on me. Gotta go, I'll be late for school.'

'Get a life.'

'I'm trying to,' shouted Joey as he ran off to school.

Chapter 3 – In the City - Graffiti

Luke was panicking. He didn't think he had the energy left for a last-minute sprint, but as he caught sight of the ABA dodging in between the traffic he picked up his pace. Rounding the corner of his block, he was frightened they might still be gaining on him. The front door had been damaged weeks ago and the Caretaker had still not repaired the lock, so he hurriedly pushed open the door. He decided to take the lift. Luckily his elderly neighbour was getting out, so he charged past him, jumped in and frantically pushed the button for his floor. The gang entered the building and took the stairs, but by the time they got to his floor, Luke was already in his flat. Shortly afterwards he could hear them banging and kicking the door. They were threatening to do a 'Mikey' which was a reference to someone the gang had punished by pouring petrol through his letterbox and dropping a lit match onto it. Mikey survived but his girlfriend and baby boy didn't. As a result, most of the people in the block had post boxes stuck on the outside of their flats and had blocked up their letterboxes. Eventually, one of the neighbours came out holding a machete and shouted at them to leave. They went but shouted a few insults as they left.

He kicked off his trainers in the hallway, ducked under the window in case they were still hanging around, and headed to the kitchen. He drank two full glasses of water and sat down for a few minutes to catch his breath and calm his nerves. He was stripping off to hop in the shower when he heard someone knocking at the back door. Knocking wasn't usually the ABA's style, so he approached quietly and was surprised to see through the small, frosted window the silhouette of Robbie. He opened the door and dragged him inside. Luke and Robbie met on their first day at school and had continued their friendship in the real world and online for many years.

'You alright?' He asked Luke.

'Yeah. Why wouldn't I be?'

'I've just seen the ABA chasing you.'

Luke didn't want to ask Robbie why he hadn't come to help him straight away, because he already knew the answer. Robbie talked a good fight, but he was unfit and asthmatic, and whilst he was fond of beating up smaller kids, none of the kids their age took him seriously.

'I managed to give them the slip.'

'Good, and don't worry, I taught Spud a lesson.'

Luke didn't know how to react to that but as Robbie still had a mouth full of teeth, he couldn't believe he'd actually come face-to-face with Spud. When he tried to press Robbie into explaining exactly how he had punished Spud, he clammed up. Since there was nothing he could do about it, he said he was going to take a shower, while Robbie played on the Xbox.

As the cool water ran down his body, Luke tried not to think what Damian would do if he didn't get him some cigarettes. He decided he was less afraid of the shop assistant, so he devised a rough plan. As soon as he was dressed, he asked Robbie to go with him to the shopping precinct and create a bit of a diversion while he got hold of as many packets as possible. Robbie agreed on the condition that they would share whatever they got equally.

After making sure the ABA was not hanging around, they left the flats by the fire escape. Luke didn't have time to notice the graffiti today, so didn't see the latest amendments, which would be sure to infuriate Spud.

Heading towards the bus stop they passed a hairdressing salon; a kickboxing gym; and a Vape bar where Robbie had spent many hours loitering and contemplating his future lungs. Several girls at school were now regularly vaping, but there were fewer lads due to the impact on testosterone levels.

They paid their fares and sat at the back of the bus, fidgeting slightly, full of nervous excitement and resentment. Luke was annoyed that he had caved into Damian's demand for more cigs and was determined to mention it to his mum when Damian wasn't around. As the bus pulled up near the precinct they went to the front and jumped off as soon as the doors opened. They headed for one of the smaller newsagents outside the main shopping centre, which from previous experience was the only one they knew of that didn't have CCTV. The plan was that Robbie would go to the back of the shop and shake up a fizzy drink, then let it explode all over the newspapers and magazines. Whilst the shop assistant was trying to deal with the mess, Luke would reach over the counter and grab as many packets of cigarettes as possible for Damian and Robbie, then leave before she noticed him.

Luke hovered near the front of the shop, looking at the bags of sweets. As soon as the young girl ran to the back, he checked around to make sure there was no one nearby. He was too fearful to go around the back of the till in case he got locked inside, so he had to literally throw himself over the desk and grab half a dozen long packs. Shoving them in his backpack and wiping the sweat out of his eyes, he scuttled out onto the pavement.

By the time the assistant had noticed that some of the shelves were empty and that lower down where the expensive stock was stacked, they would be gone.

Robbie had bustled out as quickly as possible and Luke shouted at him to run. But as Robbie was running down the road the assistant came out of the shop. Luke ran but Robbie, who was a regular twenty-cigs-a-day lad, was no match for her. She soon caught up with him and grabbed his hood. Luke heard Robbie arguing that he hadn't taken anything, but she used some kind of walkie-talkie to contact security staff in the area.

Luke hesitated and the shop assistant shouted at someone to stop him. A man wearing a Man City hoody tried to grab him, but he managed to dodge him. In the confusion, he ran headlong into a pram holding a small child and knocked the whole thing over. The kid must have banged her head quite badly as she started bawling.

Luke was terrified. He couldn't afford to be in trouble with the police again; his mum would kill him. Robbie was urging him to run away. He turned and ran back to the bus station. He hopped on the first bus back to his flat in Ardwick and sat at the back dividing up the spoils. He placed Robbie's half in a carrier bag and kept the remainder in another one and hoped it would be enough to keep Damian quiet for a while. He hadn't managed to get hold of any whisky because the newsagents didn't sell alcohol, but he hoped a big bundle of cigs would be enough to keep him happy. As the bus stopped, he checked around for members of the ABA, and as the coast was clear he made his way to his flat.

Soon after he arrived home Robbie texted to let him know that the police had let him go with a reprimand, as he didn't have any stolen property on him. He hadn't given the police Luke's name but as they had been caught together in the past it would probably only be a matter of time before they identified him, probably from CCTV in the bus station.

He slumped down on the end of his bed, feeling frustrated. They'd been so close to getting away with it. He flicked on his Xbox and loaded Call of Duty, but his mind kept wandering back to the newsagents. He was finding it difficult to concentrate although his favourite game usually kept him occupied for hours.

He was almost relieved when he heard Damian slam the front door, and the familiar sound of him hanging his leather coat up in the hallway. As Luke grabbed the bag of cigs and was about to leave his bedroom, he heard someone ring the doorbell. Damian answered the door in his usual vile humour. 'What do you want?' he demanded.

'I'd like Luke to come down to the station and answer some questions, please,' PC Jenkins said. Luke's heart sank as he recognised PC Jenkins' voice.

'What about?'

'I believe he was involved in an incident at Mason's Newsagents earlier today with Robert Sumner-Smith.'

'Robbie Sumner-Shit is a lying scumbag; he's always trying to get Luke in trouble.' Luke knew that Damian wouldn't say this out of loyalty and that it would just be a tactic to stall the police officer long enough for Luke to get rid of any evidence. He didn't like Luke, but he liked the police even less.

'I have reason to believe that Luke was shoplifting, and I would like to search these premises.'

'There won't be any stolen goods here. Go round to Robbie's place and search there,' said Damian.

'We've already searched Robbie and he didn't have anything on him. And since we have sufficient reason to believe that Luke has something, we have come armed with a warrant,' said PC Jenkins as he pushed past him. 'Don't worry I know which is Luke's room.'

Luke quickly sat on the end of his bed with his back to the door, pretending to listen to music on his phone. The police officer pulled one of his earphones out and shouted, 'I have reason to believe that you were shoplifting earlier today. I wish to search these premises. I will officially caution you, a process you're already familiar with, then take you down to the station for questioning.'

Luke tried to act nonchalant as his bedroom was systematically searched.

'Right, there's obviously nothing here, so you can sod off,' said Damian.

'Always so pleasant, aren't you, Damian? That session at charm school has really paid off.' Said PC Jenkins.

Upon hearing the conversation at the front door, Luke had quickly opened his window and thrown the cigarettes out. This is where the other police officer noticed them raining down from the third floor and had collected them in an evidence bag. He had run up the stairs to the flat and held up the bag to display the contents.

'My colleague has found these packets of cigarettes outside which match the description of the stuff stolen from Mason's.'

'Where did you find those?' Damian demanded.

'They were on the floor outside, and I'm guessing it's underneath Luke's window,' he replied.

'They're not mine,' said Luke.

'Well, they won't have your fingerprints all over them, will they?' Asked the PC who appeared to be genuinely disappointed with Luke.

The police officer read him his rights and took him, and Damian, down to the police station. Luke had already given his fingerprints in a previous incident, so they didn't have to go through that procedure again.

'The cigarettes will be tested, and if they are found to have your fingerprints on them, you'll be charged under the Theft Act 1968 with shoplifting and assault occasioning actual bodily harm. We will contact you when we get the results back, and then you will be sent a letter confirming the date that you have to appear at the local magistrate's court.'

Chapter 4 – In the Village - The Meeting

In Rowan Joey was preparing a pan of stew for dinner while James was revising for his upcoming environmental exams at college. It was well after six when his dad arrived home, and as soon as they sat down to eat Joey told him about the discussion he had heard on the radio.

'We want to come to the meeting tonight - it might get interesting, and we haven't got anything else to do.' Said Joey

'I don't expect it to be all that interesting, you'll probably be disappointed.' Replied his dad.

'I hope there's a punch-up between William and Reg. William would be bound to win, even if he is older.' Said Joey.

'I doubt it'll come to blows, but I'm sure there'll be a heated argument. I haven't spoken to a single villager who actually wants the development to go ahead.' Said his dad.

'Why don't you want it to go ahead, Dad? It's only going to be a few houses and there's loads of empty land around here,' asked James.

'I know there is, but the plan is to build from the edge of the village and out along the main road. They would go straight through the cross-country running route and take up William's lower fields and the pitches. Can you imagine not having somewhere to play football or rugby against Llugwy and the other teams around here?'

'Where will we play then?' Joey wanted to know.

'Reg is suggesting we share Llugwy's pitches and take it in turns to play at home, Said Paul.

'But they hate us, so that would be awkward,' said Joey.

'I know. But Reg has never played football or rugby, and he's only lived in the village for a few years, so he hasn't really thought it through.'

'Oh, that's worse than I thought. Well, we still want to come. We were going to run down to the village and run back afterwards so that we can do a bit more training,' said Joey

'Yeah, and maybe if I give you a head start, you'll stand a chance of beating me,' quipped James.

'It's just a matter of time,' responded Joey.

'Exactly! Your time is slower than mine,' said James.

Joey couldn't help noticing the framed pictures of James completing last year's cross-country race. The brothers were to take part in the annual race together for the first time that year. He dreamed of having his photo alongside James, both holding a medal. James had been racing for a few years, and their dad Paul had participated until the previous year. He was a local champion. The race was in a few months and James was expected to do well in it. People from all of the local villages took part, and there was a lot of rivalry between Rowan and Llugwy. Everyone was convinced that Huw Morgan, a local swindler who had been involved in credit card fraud in the past, who came from Llugwy, cheated during his last race and won it illegally, but no one worked out how, so they would love James to beat Huw's son Lloyd this year.

As they set off running, Joey mentioned the London Marathon that he had seen brief clips of on the news.

'I'd love to do something like that one day,' said Joey.

'Well, it probably takes years of training, and I don't think it pays,' said James.

'It sounded like some of the runners do it for a living,' said Joey.

'Really? That's interesting. Do they get prize money?'

'Yeah, and sponsorship.'

As they were both determined to beat the other, they stopped talking and ran at full pace to the Village Hall. James won by a few seconds.

Practically the whole village had turned out for the council meeting to discuss the proposed planning permission. The Chairman of the local council, Reg, was a big, ruddy-faced man who used every opportunity to talk about his mother who among her copious talents could bake cakes to compete with Mary Berry, made all her own clothes, had flown planes during WWII, whilst everyone who listened doubted if he even had a mother.

Catherine, who helped with the administration of the council meetings, as well as running the local shop, had opened the meeting by greeting everyone with '*Noswaith dda*' (good evening) and had invited Reg to show a PowerPoint presentation to the villagers. The computer-generated images made the development look as if it would be bringing as many trees as houses to the area.

'It's my opinion that this village has remained as a backwater for far too long,' said Reg.

An anonymous heckler shouted, 'well you're free to leave this backwater if that's how you see it.'

'But I don't wish to leave. I simply want to change the village to bring it into the twenty-first century.'

There were several expletives aimed at Reg.

Reg seemed genuinely surprised at the level of animosity.

'This development will improve the village, not detract from it.'

Paul said, 'I find that hard to believe. How many locals will be able to afford these houses?'

'We can insist that a proportion are classed as affordable and therefore at least twenty per cent cheaper,' said Reg.

'Well, what about the cross-country run?' Asked Paul.

'Unfortunately, the route will be impeded, but it can be rerouted easily enough!'

William wanted to know about the pitches.

'We're nearly at the end of the season. And next season's games can be played at Llugwy; I've already cleared that with the head of the Council there,' replied Reg.

'My father and grandfather played rugby here. Paul holds the record for the most tries scored in one game.' Argued William.

'That's ancient history,' Reg responded.

'What?' Shouted William, who had lived every one of his sixty years in the village. 'You may not be interested in the history of this village but that's because you're a newcomer. You're practically English.' There was a

27

sharp inhale from the crowd and a few nervous giggles. This was one of the worst insults you could make to a Welshman.

Reg jumped up and standing in front of his table thundered 'How dare you? My family has lived in Wales for at least fifty years.'

'Maybe so, but with a surname like Russell, you can't really be Welsh.'

'I was born in Rhyl actually. And what has my name got to do with anything?'

'Isn't a rustler someone who steals cattle and sheep? And now you want to take our land too.'

Reg took a step towards William at which point William stood up. Then with a clattering of chairs, the rest of the villagers followed suit behind him. Reg decided to retreat back behind his table.

Feeling slightly braver standing next to Catherine, Reg replied, 'As a matter of fact it's from the French Roussel, meaning little red one.'

To which Catherine replied, 'Were they referring to your nose?'

Everyone laughed, and William came back with, 'The first option sounded manlier.'

The arguments continued for several minutes. But when individuals started speaking in Welsh and aiming expletives at Reg including the use of *Twll dîn pob Sais*, meaning down with the English! (or more literally 'an arsehole every Englishman'), Catherine decided that she would have to call for order. She announced that it would have to be put to a vote. When she asked who supported

28

the proposed plans, Reg put his hand up along with five or six others.

Catherine asked who was opposed to the plan, and ten or eleven people put their hands up.

Reg explained that these plans would be amended to take into consideration some of their views and that there would be a further meeting shortly.

Then the meeting degenerated into a huge argument.

Chapter 5 - In the City – Red Diesel

When Luke got home his mum had already heard what had happened from one of the neighbours. She was pacing up and down the kitchen and demanded to know why he had stolen the cigarettes. Damian was glaring at him over her shoulder, and he was struggling to come up with a convincing lie. In the end, she shouted at him to get to bed and said they would talk in the morning.

He left the room but listened outside as Damian tried to pacify her with his 'boys will be boys' line. He then tried to change the conversation by telling her about Robbie's dad, Andrew Sumner Smith who he used to work for and was now the foreman on a building site. He would be able to get hold of some red diesel cheaply to sell to the taxi drivers. Beth had pleaded with him not to get involved in anything criminal and he convinced her that as he was paying for the diesel, it was practically legal. The diesel was left over from a previous building site that had been completed, and the company Andrew was working for was waiting for permission for the building of some new houses at Rowan, a village just inside Wales. 'I wouldn't be surprised if it has been nicked,' thought Luke as he went to bed.

Damian left for work early the next morning to collect the red diesel, whilst Beth and Luke sat down and had breakfast together, something they hadn't done for ages. 'So, tell me exactly what happened and why you stole those cigs,' his mum said.

'Mum, you don't want to know.'

'Yes I do, and I want the truth,' she demanded.

'Well, do you promise not to go mad?' he pleaded.

'As long as you've got a good reason, and I want to know who made you do it. I know you don't smoke, so you weren't pinching them for yourself.'

Luke took a deep breath and said, 'Mum, they were for Damian.'

'Don't you lie to me, lad. Damian may not be a saint, but he's helped with the mortgage, he bought a new boiler when ours broke down, and he's got a job and a car, which is more than your real dad has ever done,' she shouted.

'I'm not lying, Mum, honest. They were for Damian; he made me do it,' said Luke.

'I'm not listening to you; you're a liar as well as a thief. I bet it was Robbie, I don't know why you hang around with him. He's a complete waste of space!' she spat.

'What about Damian? You could do better than that useless bastard.'

'He's not useless. He's funny and kind. And we're not talking about Damian, we're talking about Robbie. Why do you let him intimidate you?'

'For God's sake! He doesn't intimidate me.'

'Then why do you let him get you into trouble all the time?'

'He doesn't. It was Damian. I got scared, mum.'

'Oh, come off it. I don't believe you're scared of Damian.'

'I'm not. I'm scared of what I might do to him one of these days.' He nervously chewed his fingernail.

'What the hell do you mean?'

'Remember what happened with Dad.'

'You hit your dad because he pushed me down the stairs. Damian has never hurt me.'

'He's not the saint you think he is.'

'I'm not listening to this. I'm going to work.' She wiped her eyes and stormed out, leaving him to finish his breakfast alone. It was the first nice morning they had had in ages, and she had spoiled it by taking Damian's side. He didn't know what to do, so he decided that going to school was preferable to hanging around at home feeling rubbish.

As he left his flat, he heard a commotion. One of the local kids shouted up to him, 'Have you seen what someone has done to the mural?' He didn't stop to have a conversation but ran down the back stairs to see for himself. Where it had been predominantly red, it was now sky blue. And where it had previously said MUFC, it had been subtly changed to MCFC (Manchester City Football Club). 'Oh my God! Spud is going to kill them.' Luke thought. Whoever was responsible hadn't felt proud enough of their contribution to leave their tag.

Luke took a picture of the artwork with his mobile and texted it to Robbie. Luke, surprised not to receive an immediate response, ran round to Robbie's block and took the stairs two at a time up to his front door.

'Well, what do you think?' He asked Robbie, as soon as he opened the door.

'It's not bad.'

'You what?'

'Well, it's not as if we're big United fans, is it? Why should we care?'

'Rather a red than a blue, any day of the week.'

'I'm not bothered either way. It's not as if we can afford to go to a game at Old Trafford or the Etihad, is it?'

'So? Can you imagine what Spud is going to say?'

'Who cares? He's with the ABA.'

'Just as we thought things might calm down, after some of them being banged up for the Mikey saga, we'll end up with a massive turf war again, where the ABA will be carrying knives and knuckledusters.'

'Well, we'll just have to watch our backs.'

'I'm not going to start carrying a knife. Anyway, as long as the ABA is looking for whoever did that, we'll be okay.'

'Yeah, suppose so,' said Robbie nervously.

They arrived at school in time for registration and then went straight to their PE lesson. Luke knew that Robbie would use his asthma as an excuse to sit on the bench and watch the others. The last time he had taken part in the lesson he had spent half an hour afterwards alternately puffing on a cigarette and his inhaler.

They were doing a cross-country run today, Luke's favourite activity. It gave him an opportunity to run, without having a security guard or the ABA behind him. He quickly laced up his trainers and stood beside Mr Strachan.

By nine o'clock the police had received the results of the fingerprint tests. They went to Luke's house first as he was a known persistent truant. They then called at the

33

school.   They arrived just minutes after Luke had gone running with the rest of his class.

Chapter 6 – In the Village – Joey Helps with Lambing

Joey was enjoying a good night's sleep when he heard banging on the front door. He ran downstairs and recognised William's profile through the glass panel. He opened the door and asked him what the problem was.

'I've been up most of the night with the sheep. A couple of them are in labour and they're struggling. I wondered if your dad or James could come and help me. The vet's helping out over at Meredith's farm and can't come over for at least a couple of hours.'

James couldn't afford to be late today; he had exams this week. Joey would have to go himself.

'I'll just get my dad, and I'll come with you,' he volunteered. He had often helped out on the nearby farms picking potatoes, mucking out horses, and picking the fruit that William sold to Catherine. He had helped William mind the sheep but hadn't done much lambing, although he had a vague idea of what had to be done.

He went into his dad's bedroom and woke him up.

'Dad, William needs you. A few of his sheep are having problems, can you come and help?'

'Oh, of course. Just give me a minute to get dressed.' He replied groggily.

Joey pulled on a warm sweater and his old trousers and ran downstairs. He jotted a quick note to James so he wouldn't be wondering where they were, then dashed down the path with William and his dad.

There was a mist hanging over the fields, and they saw the breath in front of their faces. They had to physically pick up one of the sheep and carry it into the barn. Joey rushed on ahead and grabbed a bale of hay, then breaking it up with a pitchfork, he placed it around the ewe. She was very quiet, and Joey was concerned about her. He tried to make her as comfortable as possible, but she was still struggling to deliver the lamb.

Eventually, William decided that they would have to help by manually pulling the lamb out by its front legs. He looked at Joey.

'Well, you've got the smallest hands.'

'But I've never done anything like that before.'

'We can't wait for the vet. What you have to do is put your hands inside the sheep, and then tie some rope around the lamb's legs.'

Feeling a bit uneasy, Joey did as he was asked. It was pretty difficult to find the legs as everything was covered in thick mucus. Eventually, he managed to tie a kind of knot and watched as William tugged on the rope. As the lamb popped out with a slight whooshing sound, Paul was ready with some straw to wipe around its mouth and nose to clear the mucus. The lamb wasn't showing any sign of life, so William gently swung it by its back legs a few times and rubbed its chest with a bit of straw until it started taking its first few breaths. They placed the lamb with its mother, and leaving Joey with them, William and Paul went back up to the field to get the other ewe that was in labour. Luckily it wasn't quite as heavy as the first one, so they made quite good progress carrying it to the barn.

The flock of sheep had been covered by the ram in stages so that they would give birth in groups of no more than five or six a day.   They moved it to the other side, away from the first sheep, and almost as soon as they put her down, the young lamb started to make an appearance. Joey was relieved; he was hoping to avoid a repetition of the first lambing.

As he ran out of the barn and down the road to his own house, Joey saw Tommo in the distant field and wondered what he was doing. What young lad would be wandering fields first thing in the morning? Joey wanted to avoid him, so he ducked down and tried to run towards the hedgerow for cover.

Tommo spotted him and started walking towards him. Joey said hello and Tommo shouted something back. As he got closer Joey noticed that Tommo seemed a bit confused.

'Have you got any money on you?' Asked Tommo.

'No' replied Joey.

'Well, I'll come home with you,' said Tommo.

Feeling slightly awkward Joey replied, 'I've only got ten quid.'

'That'll do,' answered Tommo.

Joey let Tommo into the hallway and then went upstairs for the money. He didn't really want to lend it to him but couldn't think of a reason not to. When he ran downstairs, he found Tommo in the living room. Tommo snatched the money, muttered thanks and left.

Chapter 7 – In the City – Cross Country Run

Luke had been given the usual responsibility of leading the group of runners through Ardwick, as he was the only kid in the class who was remotely interested in running. Mr Strachan was to run at the back of the group to ensure there were no stragglers. They followed the usual route out of the school via the playing fields and soon merged onto Hyde Road, then through Ardwick Green Park with its military memorial, bandstand and pond but had to pause for the traffic to cross Dolphin Street. Then after two laps of the park, they were all too soon returning to school. Luke and two of his classmates were still running, but most of the others were walking the last part of the course.

'Well done, Luke, that was excellent. You completed that in a decent time,' said Mr Strachan when he had finally managed to round everyone up and herd them into the changing rooms.

Luke was feeling pleased with himself until Robbie came over and told him the police had been to school for him.

'They're coming back at lunchtime. What do you want to do?'

Luke was hoping Mr Strachan hadn't overheard Robbie. 'Well, I'll just have to go with them. There's nothing else I can do, is there?'

Mr Strachan interrupted and wanted to know why the police were going to come back to see him. Luke tried to think of a good way to explain the situation, but in the end, decided on the truth.

'I got caught nicking some cigs, sir.'

'Why would you do something so stupid, lad? Don't tell me you've started smoking?'

'No, they weren't for me, they were for my stepdad.'

'Well, they can't speak to you without a responsible adult present. I've got a free period next; do you want me to come with you?'

Luke thought about the alternatives - asking his Mum or Damian to come out of work.

'I'm not bothered. You can come if you like.' Secretly praying that Mr Strachan would come with him.

'I don't *like* actually. I'm doing you a favour.'

'Okay. Thanks.'

'Anyway, it will probably reflect better on you if you go now voluntarily, rather than wait for them to come and pick you up.'

'But it will look better if everyone sees him being picked up by the police,' interrupted Robbie.

'I doubt that,' said Mr Strachan.

'Course it will, it will give him cred,' said Robbie.

Mr Strachan glared at him but didn't reply. Then he spoke to Luke, 'Let me just go and get a permission slip to take you out of school and make sure someone can cover my first lesson after lunch, in case it takes a bit longer than expected.'

When he had gone Robbie rounded on Luke. 'Why the hell are you going with him? He'll only want to know all your business.'

'No, he won't. He's just trying to help.'

'He probably just wants to get out of PE. He must hate it as much as we do.'

'I don't hate PE. You do.'

Mr Strachan came out of the staff room at that moment. He noticed Robbie with his mouth opening and closing like a fish out of water. He walked out to the car park with Luke nervously following him. He had never been out of school on his own with a teacher before and was wondering what to talk about.

Once they were in the car Mr Strachan asked Luke if he had a good relationship with his stepdad.

'Well we've never had a fight or anything, but we don't talk much.'

'And if you hadn't agreed to get the cigarettes, do you think it would have led to a fight?'

'Only if he kept pushing me around.'

'Have you ever fought before?'

'No.'

'So why are you worried that it would end in a fight on this occasion?'

'Because of what happened with my dad.'

On the way to the police station, they went past the back of a disused warehouse. Spud had written his tag in enormous red and white letters several months beforehand. Recently an enterprising mobile catering unit had benefited from adding the word "Baked" before it, with the letter "s" at the end of Spud, and underneath they had written "next left". Even in the pouring rain, it was equal to any of the huge billboard advertisements in the area for being eye-catching and getting its point across.

After waiting for what felt like an interminable length of time, Mr Strachan prompted him to tell him what had happened with his dad.

Luke could barely get his thoughts straight in his head, but he falteringly told his story.

'I hit my dad with a snooker cue.'

After a sharp intake of breath, Mr Strachan asked why.

'I didn't know what else to do.'

'Couldn't you have called the police, your mum, a neighbour?'

'There wasn't time. It all happened very fast.'

'What happened?'

After keeping everything bottled up for so long, Luke was relieved to find someone he could talk to. 'My dad punched my mum in the stomach and pushed her down the stairs. He was pissed off because he had just found out she was pregnant, and he didn't think he could be the dad as he had only been out for a couple of months.'

'Out?'

Luke nodded in the direction of Strangeways prison which could be seen in the distance.

'He's back inside now.'

Mr Strachan prompted him to continue.

'I was so scared that he was going to kill her that I picked up his snooker cue and hit him across the head with it. One of the neighbours called the police and I was charged with grievous bodily harm. I honestly thought he'd make the police drop the charges when everything

42

had calmed down, but he couldn't. It had to go to court because it was a serious assault.'

'Didn't they take all that into consideration?' Asked Mr Strachan.

'Oh yes, they knew he was no saint and that's probably what kept me out of a young offenders' institute. But I've now got a charge of violent conduct on my record.' He still had nightmares about the incident and thought his mum probably did too.

'My mum refused to press charges against him, as he convinced her to take him back. And I think she was too scared anyway.' Luke could still remember the phrases his dad had used to convince his mum the argument was all her fault for making him jealous. She stood by him all through his trial and it was only when he was sent to prison that she finally scraped together enough confidence to apply for a divorce. Months later, after meeting Damian on a dating website, she thought she had finally found a decent, hard-working man.

Chapter 8 – In the Village – The Incentive

Feeling uneasy after his run-in with Tommo earlier that morning, Joey was struggling to pay attention to any of his lessons. He only really started listening when his teacher, Mr Martin, brought up the subject of the new houses.

'I've been reading some documents on the internet and the Government is deliberately giving incentives to those who build new houses.' Mr Martin told the class.

'Why would they do that?' Joey wanted to know.

'Apparently, there is a massive demand for more housing. I'll show you something on the computer which proves what the Government is doing.'

Mr Martin found a statement from The Communities Secretary which said "Government targets will offer powerful incentives so that people see the benefits of building new homes. This will ensure those local authorities that take action now to consent and support the construction of new homes will receive a direct and substantial benefit for their actions. These incentives will be a priority."

'But will they be allowed to put them on William's land?'

'Yes, because he probably leases some of the lower fields, so the Council can simply reclaim them.'

Joey walked home with a heavy heart. When he got home James was already preparing dinner. He tried to broach the subject with James but he cut him short.

'Can't we just forget about that for one night? Why don't you get your homework done and we can have a quick run after dinner? Dad said he might be home early tonight.'

'Alright, but will you help me with my maths. I hate maths.'

'Okay,' James promised as he placed a cottage pie in the oven.

When Paul came in Joey nearly brought up the subject of the statement from the Communities Secretary, but James stopped him with a glance. They ate their dinner sat at the old oak table in the kitchen. Then James reminded Joey to get changed.

'Come on, Joey, we've got the cross-country run to train for. Don't forget that dad let the family down badly a couple of years ago, so it's up to us to restore the family honour.'

'Hey, I won that race fair and square, but I couldn't prove that Huw Morgan cheated. I still haven't worked out how he did it. There were marshalls all the way around the course,' said his dad.

'Maybe he blackmailed someone to turn a blind eye,' suggested Joey.

'I don't think anyone here is likely to be open to blackmail,' his dad replied.

'What about Reg? Maybe Huw saw him doing something wicked and now he's making his life a misery!' Replied Joey.

'I'm sure that if anyone was going to blackmail Reg, they would want a lot more than to win the cross-country race,' replied dad.

'That's true; perhaps Huw was just a better athlete,' joked James.

Joey pulled on his running shoes and together he and James went out to run the entire course. Their dad was going down to where the finish line would be, with a stopwatch. He had finished the course in an hour and six minutes last time. James expected to be able to do it in a similar time and Joey in a few minutes more.

Joey impatiently did his stretches and surveyed the course. He could see most of it from where he stood. It was arduous and crisscrossed over three hills. The path was a bit rocky and narrow in parts and there were several obstacles along the way. They would have to cross the river twice over rickety footbridges, climb three stiles, dodge the swampy parts of the lower fields and avoid any sheep along the way.

It was a nice spring evening with a cool breeze blowing. Joey kept pace with James until three-quarters way around the course, then on the final hill, James pulled away. He was several metres ahead, but the early advantage was lost when they were running downhill. James was more cautious, but Joey tore down the hill. He made up quite a bit of the difference, but on the last long straight as Joey was tiring slightly, James again pulled away and finished a couple of minutes ahead. Paul was at the finishing line with his stopwatch.

'I don't believe it; you finished two minutes faster than my best time. There must be something wrong with this stopwatch,' said Paul shaking it theatrically.

'Just face it, old man, I beat you fair and square,' said James.

'Oh yeah, oh yeah, oh yeah,' chanted Joey.

'Did you say that you were going to treat us to lunch at the weekend at the new pub restaurant if we beat your time?' Asked James.

'I didn't, but as you've both worked so hard lately, I think you deserve it. But you have to choose the cheapest items on the menu and buy your own drinks,' he joked.

Chapter 9 — In the City – The Police Station

As Luke and Mr Strachan pulled up outside the police station, two police cars shot past them with their sirens blaring. The screeching noise added to Luke's nerves. When they got inside the police station, Luke stood to one side trying to read one of the posters on the wall, warning about the dangers of using unlicensed taxis. However, he couldn't concentrate on what it said. He tried to distract himself but felt nervous and embarrassed. Mr Strachan approached the desk and spoke to the duty sergeant.

'This is Luke Mills. He's wanted with reference to an offence. Can we speak to PC Jenkins please?'

They took a seat and eventually PC Jenkins arrived and took them through to a small room. Mr Strachan introduced himself and explained that he would be acting as a responsible adult, in the absence of Luke's mum or stepfather. PC Jenkins acknowledged Mr Strachan and thanked Luke for coming to the station and reminded him he was still under caution. He reiterated that they had tested the cigarettes which were found outside his flat, and they were found to have his fingerprints on them. As the value of the cigarettes was several hundred pounds it could not be dealt with as a minor offence. He also told him that the mother of the little girl wanted to press charges as her daughter had been required to have four sutures to the cut on her forehead and would be scarred. This was a much more serious charge than the shoplifting offence and he would be required to attend court. He reminded Luke of his list of previous minor offences, as well as the charge for violent conduct. He recommended that when it went to court, he would do well to plead guilty.

Mr Strachan asked if he could have a quick word outside.

Luke tried to listen and heard Mr Strachan ask some questions regarding the actual procedure and mentioned that Luke was generally a good lad who didn't get into trouble at school.

'Well he's had a more colourful career out of school,' replied PC Jenkins.

'That may be as a result of outside influences,' said Mr Strachan.

'Do you mean the gang he's in?'

'No, I didn't know he was in a gang. I was thinking of his stepfather. Are you familiar with him?'

'Oh yes, he's one of our frequent flyers. Damian is so well known to us that we only use his first name.'

'Well, I hope you take his home environment into consideration.'

'The courts will decide on the appropriate punishment.'

Luke was feeling pretty uneasy as they drove back to school. Eventually, Mr Strachan broke the silence by telling Luke that the least he could expect would be Community Service.

'What sort of stuff do you think I'll have to do?'

'Probably litter picking, gardening or cleaning up graffiti.'

Luke was reminded of the recent additions to the street art at home and told Mr Strachan about it.

'That isn't art, it isn't clever, it's vandalism.'

'You've seen the estate where I live, haven't you?'

'Yes, and?'

'It's bloody ugly. Just grey concrete blocks. It's like a prison, and we haven't done anything wrong.'

Mr Strachan raised an eyebrow.

'Well my mum has never broken any laws, and I'm sure plenty of the other people who live there haven't either. At least the graffiti is interesting.'

'People daubing their names everywhere is not interesting, Luke. It's criminal damage.'

'It's not just tags, it really is art. Come and see it if you don't believe me.'

'I'm not interested, Luke. And you really shouldn't get involved in any of that.'

'I don't do any of it. I wouldn't dare. It kind of unofficially belongs to Spud and he's with the ABA.'

'And that's another thing. You don't want to get drawn into gangs. Look at what has happened to kids who've got sucked into all that violence and trouble.'

'I'm not really in a gang, but Robbie likes to convince everyone we are.'

'What do you mean, you're *not really* in a gang? The police seem to think you are.'

'We're just kids but we've formed a gang so that we don't have to join someone else's.'

Mr Strachan appeared to be quite impressed with this. 'Who is in your gang?'

'Me, Robbie, his kid brother Scott, Prowsey, Kyle, Duje, Che, Ibra, Ains, Lyan, Strongarms, Nathan, Mo, Baz, Will, Rom and Jonesy.'

'And what do you have to do to become a member of this gang?'

'Nothing, but we tell everyone that they have to go up to someone wearing a City shirt and stab them. Nobody wants to do that, so they don't join our gang.'

'What's the name of this non-existent gang?'

'We're called The Ardwick Hardmen.'

'It's a clever idea, but it might be braver to just shun all gangs, rather than pretend it's cool.'

'That wouldn't be brave, it would be suicidal. Can you imagine me and Robbie going up to the ABA and saying, "We shun your gang"?'

Mr Strachan laughed and said, 'Probably not.'

As they pulled into the school car park Mr Strachan asked Luke what his next lesson was.

'Err I'm not sure.'

'Don't tell me, you bunk off after PE! You have got to stop doing that. It's time to grow up now and stop wasting your education.'

'What good is an education to me? What can I possibly do for a job?'

'I don't know, but I'm certain that your choices will be a lot better if you get some decent qualifications. Especially maths and English.'

'I hate English. It's crap! We always have to read boring books.'

'No, you don't. Now you're in upper school you can choose most of the books you want to read.'

'Really? I didn't know that.'

'That's probably because you haven't been to a lesson for ages.'

'Well, there aren't any books I want to read.'

'How do you know? When was the last time you picked up a book?'

'Couple of years ago. I think it was something about men and mice.'

'Of Mice and Men. A brilliant story about pursuing the American Dream. A terribly sad twist at the end.'

'Really? I don't remember any of that.'

'Well you should read "Twin Ambitions"- it's the Mo Farah story. He's a fantastic marathon runner who came from Somalia as a young lad.'

'That's the old bloke who won the marathon a couple of weeks ago. I didn't know runners could write books too.'

'He's not that old, he's younger than me.'

'Yeah?' Luke was aiming for innocent but fell short and landed on impudent.

'Yes, and he could teach you a thing or two about running. And despite his poor start in life, he's managed to become a superstar.'

'Really? How did he do that? Just from running?'

'Yes. I can't talk now.'

'Please, just tell me how?'

'Get to your next lesson. I've got to go and take over from Mr Kaminsky who is looking after my year eight students. I don't know who I feel most sorry for.'

'Year eight. Rocky is terrifying.'

'Why do they call him Rocky, he's never boxed as far as I know.'

'He once said his name means rock or stone. Can't you just tell me a bit about Farah?'

'Not now Luke. Go and get the book out of the library.'

He then ran off to relieve Mr Kaminsky, leaving Luke standing in the corridor.

Luke was late for his English lesson and as he walked into the classroom everyone turned to stare. He was embarrassed so snarled at one or two of the other kids and went and sat at the back of the room. The teacher, Miss Littleton, told the rest of the class to settle down and get on with their reading, then approached Luke.

'We're doing private reading at the moment, have you got a book?'

'Err, no.'

'Well, I can provide you with one or you can quickly pop to the library and get one out. And I mean quickly. Pick something you will enjoy because after you have read it you have to do a presentation to the rest of the class about the story and the author.'

'Okay.'

When Luke entered the library, he noticed the signs above the bookcases indicating the various categories such as History, Fiction, Romance and so on. He didn't know which group the book he wanted fell into. He wandered about aimlessly for a few minutes when the librarian approached him.

'Can I help you?'

'Yes. I want a book about a marathon runner.'

'Right, and what's his name?'

'Err, Mo Farah.'

'Let me check on the system'

She went around the desk and started typing into the computer.

'Do you know what it's called?'

'Oh yeah, "Twin Ambitions".'

She typed in a few search words and found the book he was referring to. As she was locating it he looked around at the huge number of sports books available. He thought he might come back at some point and see if there was anything that might give him a clue about a future job. She stamped the inside of the book and told him it needed to be returned within two weeks. He went back to his English lesson and surprised himself and everyone around him by putting his head down and reading.

Chapter 10 – In the Village – The Hut

Joey was worried that the new houses would destroy the route used for the annual race and decided to do some research and check out other villages where houses had been built in the last few years. When he had passed new housing estates, he thought they looked quite tidy, particularly compared to some of the old, dilapidated farmyards. But then he realised that they didn't look 'Welsh' somehow. He couldn't say what was wrong with them exactly, except they were identical. In Rowan, the postman would be able to deliver the letters accurately if the envelopes contained no address at all and only a brief description of the property. For example, William's old farmhouse with the overgrown driveway and a tractor growing in the yard; Fred's pristine white house; Jones the phones (he worked for a telecoms company) with the Welsh flag outside where someone had put a smiley face on the dragon; Catherine's shop and café with the red awnings; next door to Gavin's sky-blue cottage.

He was almost looking forward to the next meeting. In the meantime, he would go for a run to clear his head. He set off up the hill towards William's farm, running through the field where Puffing Billy, the huge black bull was grazing, and across the stream. It was freezing cold and his feet were soaking. He ran as far as the ancient rowan tree, after which the village was rumoured to have been named. The path was gravelly and a bit slippery and he lost his footing a few times. When he reached the top of the hill, he stopped to catch his breath. He could see William with his sheepdog Dylan checking his sheep. Then in the distance, he could see someone in a red hoody stumbling about. Joey thought it might be James' college hoody. James should be in college, so he decided to find out what he was up to.

He ran down into the dip in the field and climbed over the dry-stone wall. He could no longer see the red hoody wearer but thought he heard a noise coming from the deserted shepherd's hut. It was an old wooden structure that was on wheels so that it could be pulled to different fields being used by William. As William tended to use just a few fields now, the hut had been abandoned years ago, only being used occasionally for shelter by walkers or campers.

Joey approached the shed slowly. The door was closed, and nettles and weeds were growing all around it preventing him from getting near enough to clear the mud and spider webs from the window, so he couldn't see into it. He listened at the door for what seemed like an age. He was about to push the door when it was suddenly opened from inside. Tommo was blocking his view into the shed.

'What do you want?' Tommo shouted.

'Nothing. I thought I saw James,' Joey replied, taking a step back and stumbling over the weeds.

'Well you didn't, go away.'

He slammed the door so hard Joey was surprised it remained in one piece. He decided there was definitely no point in reminding him about the tenner.

Joey ran back up the hill. When he got home, he paced about nervously, jumping at every sound and wishing it was James' key in the door. When James finally did come home Joey told him of his encounter with Tommo.

'What was he doing in William's old hut?' Asked James.

'I don't know. He smelt terrible. I think he was wearing your red hoody too.'

'What? How did he get hold of it?'

'You don't think he took it when he came here asking for some money, do you? I did leave him alone for a couple of minutes.'

'Right, let's go and have a word with him.'

They put their running shoes on and alternately walked and ran down to the hut. Halfway there they saw William in his top field and for the first time that either of them could remember, they ignored him. They were twitching with adrenalin but didn't want to arrive out of breath and feel disadvantaged. They took a moment to catch their breath and tried to come up with a plan.

'There are two of us and only one of him,' said James.

'What if he's not alone? I've seen a couple of strange guys dressed in black tracksuits hanging around,' said Joey.

'Someone mentioned them at college. I thought they were making it up. Okay, well let's go for the element of surprise,' said James.

Joey, feeling stronger with James behind him, took the lead when they approached the door to the hut. He didn't bother knocking, he just swung his leg up and kicked the door open. He had his fists braced and was disappointed to find the shed empty.

They both cautiously entered, kicking over the rubbish and some industrial-type gloves scattered over the floor. There was a sleeping bag on one side, and an open cupboard held a couple of cans of lager and some cigarette-making paraphernalia. On the opposite side of the shed, creating a strange atmosphere and giving off a strong, sweet smell, were loads of little seedlings.

'What the hell are they?' Asked Joey.

'Not sure. I wonder if it's cannabis. I've never seen it in real life before.'

'Could be, it does have a distinctive five-point leaf.'

James wondered how Joey knew that but didn't follow up on the subject.

They had a quick scout around the rest of the cabin but there was nothing else there, so they went outside. They scoured the area and were secretly relieved they didn't see anyone. Then James noticed the same strange plants growing in untidy clumps just a few metres away, surrounded and camouflaged by lots of weeds and wildflowers.

'Jesus, he must be cultivating this stuff.'

Joey bent to pull some up, but James stopped him.

'Don't touch them, just in case.'

He pulled out his phone and took a picture of the area, then a close-up of the plants.

'Let's google this and find out if it is cannabis. I'm surprised it grows outdoors when it's pretty cold,' said Joey.

'Me too. Perhaps it's a hardy variety,' said James.
'You're such a geek!' Said Joey.

Chapter 11 – In the City – Graffiti gets Vandalised

It was a Saturday morning when Luke received the letter informing him of his appointment at the local Magistrate's court, and he was dreading bringing the subject up to his mum. He was anticipating her anger, but he was sure she would not make him attend alone.

'Well, I don't think I'll be able to take time off work to go with you.'

He was too proud to try and convince her so replied, 'it's alright, I can go on my own.'

'It's shameful that you're so familiar with the place. Maybe Damian could go with you.'

'NO! I don't want him to.'

'Alright, calm down. He probably doesn't want to go anyway.'

'I'll ask Robbie to come.'

'It would need to be an adult. Maybe Nan could take a day off work.'

'I might ask Mr Strachan.'

'I'm not sure that's a good idea. We don't want everyone to know our business.'

'Well, he already knows most of it. He came with me to the police station.'

'Did he? I didn't know that. Why didn't you tell me?'

'You didn't ask.'

'What?'

'Anyway, I'm off out.' He pulled the charger out of his 'phone and shoved it in his pocket. 'See you later.'

Attempting to avoid the ABA, Luke took the back stairs out of the flats and noticed that the whole mural had been covered up by a series of green and yellow stripes, with a star-spangled banner in the middle and the word Buccaneers written across it. He ran round to Robbie's flat and told him what had happened. Robbie's younger brother Scott was keen to see it for himself so together they all wandered over to the mural.

'How pathetic. At least what was there before had artistic merit,' said Robbie.

'It was a tribute to City. In what way was that artistic?' Asked Luke.

'Well, this is obviously a dig at the Glazers,' said Scott.

Robbie and Luke exchanged glances.

'What are you on about?' asked Robbie

'The artist is trying to say that the Glazers are Buccaneers because they also own the Tampa Bay Buccaneers.'

'Who?' Asked Robbie.

'They're an American football team,' said Luke.

'Why do they call it football when they mainly throw the ball to each other?' Asked Robbie.

'No idea,' said Luke.

'I need a cig,' said Robbie, 'have you got any money on you?' he asked Scott.

'Nope.'

'Yeah, you have, hand it over.'

'I haven't,' responded Scott.

Robbie tried to lash out at Scott, but he deftly dodged his fist. Then Scott did the one thing that was guaranteed to temporarily get him out of harm's way – he ran home. Unfortunately, he was almost as asthmatic as Robbie so had to keep pausing for breath.

'I got my letter today. I've got to go to court in two weeks,' said Luke.

'Oh well, at least I haven't got to come with you this time,' Robbie replied.

'Great. Thanks for the support.'

'Listen, my mum and dad would go mad if I ended up in court one more time.'

'Well, my mum is not exactly thrilled. And Damian's not taking any of the blame.'

'Well tell your mum it was him who put you up to it.'

'I did.'

'Good, about time she realised what he's really like.'

'She didn't believe me.'

'For God's sake. What is it with your mum and men?'

'No idea.'

'What do you want to do today?'

'Not bothered.'

'Got any money?'

'No, have you?'

'No, but Scott has. We can borrow that.'

'Do you mean borrow or nick?'

'Same thing.'

As they wandered over to Robbie's, Luke noticed some rough pieces of graffiti, all done in sky blue, and stencilled somehow. There were no tags on them to identify the 'artist'. They were of tall, stick men with heads like aliens, and they had voice balloons with sarcastic comments about Manchester United in them.

'Whoever did these obviously hates United,' observed Luke.

'They're not bad, are they? I think they look a bit like Banksy's,' replied Robbie.

'Banksy? The graffiti guy?'

'Yes. He's really funny. And rich.'

'How do you get rich from graffiti?'

'Don't know.'

They walked on a bit further then Robbie stopped. Luke wondered what the matter was. He waited while Robbie finally mumbled something that sounded like an invitation to go and see an exhibition. He was embarrassed to ask and kept his head down as he muttered about the fact that it would be free to get in and although there would be work from lots of artists, he was only interested in seeing Banksy's work.

'Err, not really. I like graffiti but I'd feel a bit weird wandering around an art gallery with a glass of wine.'

'I doubt they'd give us wine,'

'I'd rather not find out. Why don't you ask Scott?'

'Hmm maybe.'

'Anyway, what were you up to last night? I was on Xbox live all night and you didn't come on.'

Luke was relieved at the change of subject until he remembered what he had actually been doing. 'I was watching telly.'

'Why what was on?'

'Can't remember.'

Luke had been reading the book about Mo Farah and his amazing rise from his life in Somalia to running for Great Britain. He wasn't particularly interested in reading, but he had read quite a bit before he went to bed. He was particularly surprised by the fact that Mo had been influenced by his PE teacher who encouraged him to take part in races when he was quite young. He had almost decided to go to another English lesson when he returned to school on Monday.

When they got to Robbie's flat his mum Sandra opened the door for them.

'Why didn't you take your key?'

'I couldn't find it.'

'Typical.' She noticed Luke and scowling, returned to washing her skirting boards. She was constantly in fear of germs, or anything being untidy or out of place. On one occasion he had seen her cleaning all the door handles five or six times, which made him feel really uncomfortable.

Luke thought that Sandra's taste in clothes was quite similar to Robbie's. They both bought their clothes from sports shops and liked to insist they were the latest fashions with designer names emblazoned on them.

Robbie and Luke went straight to Scott's bedroom and found him reading a book by Stephen Hawking.

'What the hell is that?' Asked Robbie.

'It's a book about the Theory of Cosmology,' said Scott. 'Weirdo.'

Robbie asked Scott to lend him some money.

'No,' was the instant reply.

'I only want to borrow it.'

'That's what you said last time.'

'Well, what do you need money for? You haven't got any friends to go out with.'

Luke cringed at the remark.

'I'm saving up for a telescope.'

'What the hell do you want a telescope for?'

'So I can see the stars and planets at night.'

'Trust me, they will still be there in another month, so hand it over.'

'No.'

As Robbie advanced toward Scott, he ran around the other side of his bed.

'What do you need money for?' Asked Scott.

'Don't know yet. But I'm sure we'll think of something.'

'Actually Robbie, I was supposed to go round to my Nan's. I'll see you later.' Luke thought that might be the only way of stopping any potential bloodshed.

As he left the flats Luke spotted some more of the 'blue man' graffiti. It was pretty amateurish.

He decided he would have to walk around to his Nan's in case Robbie was watching him. He hadn't been to see her for a while, and he hoped she would be in. He decided to send her a quick text just in case.

'Are you in?' He decided not to use text speak, as he didn't think she would understand it.

'Y r u on yr way?' Luke laughed out loud at her response and was embarrassed when people standing at a bus stop stared at him.

'Yeah, see you in a bit.' He decided to run the rest of the way; it was only a couple of miles. As he neared her house, he decided that he would try and go for a long run later, so that he could clear his head, when it was starting to get dark. He preferred the dark evenings to do his running, and he wondered what he would do in another month or so when the evenings were light. He had printed out a training programme from the internet but had not managed to stick to it as well as he would have liked. He had recently been spending time reading the Mo Farah book, which was interesting, but he wasn't sure it would help him find a job he would actually like.

He rang the doorbell, which played 'La Cucaracha'. His Nan changed the music regularly so that at Halloween it would play the opening notes of Beethoven's Fifth Symphony, and at Christmas, it played 'Deck the Halls'.

'Hello love, come on in.'

'Hiya Nan. Have you got anything to eat, I'm starving?'

As Luke had his hand in the biscuit tin his Nan put the kettle on and made him a sandwich. He decided to wait a few minutes before telling her about the court case. He was pretty certain his mum wouldn't have mentioned it.

'So how have you been?' She asked.

'Fine. I've started running.' Luke replied.

'Why? To get away from some of the gangs on the estate?'

'Hah. No, it's just for fun at the moment until I get a bit fitter.' He paused for a moment then suddenly said, 'Then I think I'll try and enter the half-marathon.'

'But you've never done anything like that before. Why have you taken up running now?'

'I don't know. I just really enjoy it. I wish Robbie did so he could come with me.'

'He's a bit too fond of his mum's cooking I think.'

'She is a great cook. Not that she ever cooks for me, she hates me.'

'I'm sure she doesn't.'

'I'm sure she does. She blames me for getting Robbie in trouble all the time.'

'But it's usually his fault isn't it – when it isn't Damian's?'

'I know. But he's her blue-eyed boy, and she can't see what he's really like.'

They were both quiet for a moment as they pondered who she reminded them of.

'Well anyway, a half marathon? That's brilliant Luke. What does your mum think?'

It suddenly occurred to Luke that he hadn't discussed his plans with his mum. He hadn't had many worthwhile conversations with her for a while but didn't know why. They used to talk all the time, especially when his dad first went to prison. Damian seemed to be in the way somehow.

'She's fine with it.'

'Oh good. How's Damian?'

'Same as usual.'

'So, no improvement then? That's a shame.' They both laughed at the dig.

'Did mum tell you what happened?' At his Nan's blank expression, he ploughed on. 'Damian got me to nick some cigs for him and I got caught. I've got to go to court soon.'

'Oh no. Your mum must be furious.'

'She is, but as usual, she doesn't believe it was for Damian. She's convinced it was for Robbie because he was there.'

His nan looked surprised for a moment but didn't want to appear disloyal to her daughter, said 'I think she's so relieved that Damian's not violent like your dad that she'll put up with his nonsense, and completely fails to see his faults.'

Luke was relieved that someone else could actually see Damian and all his flaws. After a pause, he asked, 'Is there any chance you could come to court with me? Mum and Damian both have to work.'

'I don't think I can love. I've used up all my holidays from the Printworks. I went to bring the caravan back from Anglesey so that it could be properly cleaned and repaired for the summer.'

'Oh, okay.'

'Well, can't you go with Robbie and his parents?'

'No, Robbie isn't being charged.'

'Why not? You said he was with you.'

'He was, but I had all the cigarettes, and he was empty-handed.'

'He often manages to wriggle out of trouble. I don't know how he does it. He's not distantly related to Damian, is he?'

'I doubt it!'

'Is there anyone else you could ask to go with you?'

'Yes, I'll ask Mr Strachan. He's my PE teacher.'

'Well, if you're sure. But if he can't do it, let me know and I'll see what I can do. I might have to take a day off sick, which I'd rather not do.'

Feeling a bit cheeky Luke asked 'well, are there any jobs I could do to earn some money to pay the fine that I'll probably get?'

'You could clean the caravan for a start.'

'Alright, can I do it tomorrow before I've been for a run?'

'Of course, love.'

'I only run at night when it's dark, so the other kids can't see me.'

'Well run in the morning when they're still in bed.'

'I'll still be in bed.'

'Well get up early then, you lazy boy. You'll be surprised how nice everything is first thing in the morning.'

'I really want to believe you,' he said sceptically.

After he left his Nan's, he went straight home. As he approached the back of the flats, he could see that the graffiti had been added to. Written in the middle of the flag was '*Buccaneer: a person who is recklessly adventurous or unscrupulous, especially in business*', Luke could only guess what it meant. He wondered what Scott would make of it, not to mention Spud.

Chapter 12 – In the Village – Strange Plants

James grabbed his laptop and typed several words into the search engine. He got over 45,000 results. He clicked on the first link and an image of a similar-looking plant popped up. He read out the main details to Joey:

'Cannabis sativa. A mind-altering drug.'

'This is serious. Should we report it to the police?' Asked Joey.

'I don't know. I can't imagine our local plod will know what to do and by the time someone comes from the city anything could have happened,' said James.

'We'll need to be really careful,' said Joey.

'He's obviously growing this stuff. I wonder if he's tried selling it to anyone else.'

'Well, he does send images of dandelions and stuff on Snapchat with three words that indicate where they are. Anybody can find them using the What3Words app. They pick up the drugs and leave the cash with him watching from nearby, so he's never actually caught with loads of drugs or cash on him.'

'Damn! He's a lot more resourceful than I gave him credit for. We have to find out how to destroy the plants.'

'Without him knowing it was us.'

'Definitely.'

Their research highlighted the problem of using chemical weed killers. They could easily get into the water system; kill wildlife and damage other crops. They had to be careful as the cannabis plants were growing near

William's land and they couldn't risk hurting Puffing Billy or the sheep.

James suggested using something organic like acetic acid.

'Acid? That could be dangerous. Where would we even get hold of the stuff?'

'The kitchen. It's otherwise known as vinegar.'

'Really? You're so annoying at times. Anyway, where are we going to get hold of enough to kill so many plants?'

'We'll have to buy some from Catherine, and maybe nip into Llugwy after school.'

'Okay. I'll go and get some. You find out how to use it. Try to be subtle and if Tommo is hanging around the shop, don't buy it. He'll be suspicious after we've killed the plants because of the smell of vinegar.'

Joey jumped on his bike and took part of the mountain biking route to the shop. He tore through the gentle slopes but slowed down over the rocky bits, where he'd lost the skin off his knees in the past. His favourite area was known as Falseteeth, but he had no idea how it got its name. It was very hilly and also swerved left and right. Even though he'd ridden through it many times, he still had to give it his full attention. He rode through bracken and puddles, then into the village itself.

He went into the shop and found the biggest bottle of vinegar Catherine had. He bought some other bits and pieces and handed the items over to her. He was excited and anxious about his mission with James. As she gave him his change Joey asked her, 'It's the Council meeting tonight, are you going to it?'

'Yes, I hope your dad will be coming with you and James.

'Yes. We're looking forward to it.'

Joey was sure, after the conversations his dad and William had held with everyone, that the planning permission would never be granted.

The villagers were talking quite loudly amongst themselves and Joey sensed that their attitudes were still opposed to the development. The meeting was called to order by Catherine, who had to shout to be heard, and Reg stood up and spoke passionately about the benefits of the scheme. There would be affordable housing for residents of the village; the school would remain at Llugwy and could possibly be improved; the pitches and church would remain, and a local doctor was a strong possibility. He also mentioned that the village hall would be replaced by a new brick structure where they would be able to hold meetings for mums and tots; there would be a youth club; more regular dances; and lots of other things that he would be happy to consider.

Joey realised that most people might want all of those things. Reg asked if anyone had any questions.

'What about jobs for local people?'

'I can guarantee that the majority of the jobs will be open for local people to apply for. There will be a few specialist roles that will be filled by people already working for the development company, but the remainder will be advertised locally first and if they are not filled, they will be opened up to the nearest cities.'

'So, by the nearest cities do you mean English cities?'

'Yes, of course, Manchester, Liverpool and Chester.'

'Oh great, we'll be overrun by Sais.'

'Does it matter as long as they are skilled craftsmen and can do the job? They will be eating in the café, drinking in the pub and using B&Bs in the area.'

'How can they afford to stay in B&Bs for months at a time?'

'Well some of them might just live in caravans on the edge of the site. It's common practice on lots of building sites. Is there anything else?'

'I know you are initially asking for sixty, but where will it end? How do we know that we can trust you?' Demanded Paul.

'We have no *immediate* plans to build more than sixty houses.' Which did little to allay everyone's fears

Then raising his voice, William asked, 'Reg have you considered that this could be an Area of Outstanding Natural Beauty or a Site of Nature Conservation Importance?'

This completely threw Reg as he hadn't been expecting this level of resistance still.

'For goodness' sake, William. It's a bloody field at the end of the day, not the sweeping moorland of the Yorkshire dales! It's hardly likely to inspire prose and poetry is it?'

'We haven't had an opportunity to have the area properly analysed by experts.'

'You don't need to have it analysed by experts. I can tell you now that it is not a site of Nature Conservation Importance.'

Paul showing his solidarity with William responded with, 'Well we prefer to have our minds put at rest and I'm sure you won't mind waiting until it has been properly analysed, will you?'

'And when it has been analysed do you promise to stop making further objections?'

'No,' said William, Paul, and several other villagers rather firmly.

Reg glared at the two men at the back of the room. They stood up and got everyone's attention. The first man was tall and attractive with dark wavy hair. He introduced himself as John Miller and his foreman as Andrew Sumner-Smith.

'Well, what about the mess? You cannot build sixty houses and not turn up loads of mud. It'll make the rest of the village an eyesore. And what about the damage caused by having huge wagons travelling up and down our small roads every day?' William asked.

'Please let me give my assurance as the managing director of Millers Developers that we have never left any site messy. We will re-lay the main road as soon as we have laid all drains and so on. And I am sure you will appreciate that there are currently several nasty potholes, but its condition will be improved after we have finished.'

At this point, Reg jumped up and decided to end the meeting while everyone was thinking of all of the benefits.

'We have heard from everyone, and I'm sure we can all appreciate how much better off we all will be.'

William couldn't resist saying, 'And I'm sure you will be better off than the rest of us.'

Reg snorted and informed the villagers that this meeting was merely a courtesy to them, that their comments had been listened to, but the final decision would be made by the Councillors at their next meeting.

Joey, James and Paul piled out of the room with everyone else. There wasn't much to say as everyone was still shell-shocked.

Chapter 13 – In the City – Twin Ambitions

It was early on Monday morning and it was raining heavily. Luke had overheard Damian passing a remark to his mum about how much money he was making from selling red diesel to the taxi drivers. He couldn't understand how Damian constantly flouted the law but never got caught. He seemed to live such a charmed life; it was sickening.

After he had pulled back his curtains and glimpsed outside and seen the weather, he was considering missing school. But then he noticed the book 'Twin Ambitions' and decided the only way to change his fortunes was to try and make a bit of an effort at school. Even some of his teachers didn't appear to be completely useless. He walked quickly, in case the ABA was hanging around nearby, though early mornings were a lot rarer than late nights for them. Also, their work ethic didn't stretch to rainy evenings, which allowed Luke more opportunities to run without their added input.

After registration, he went to his English lesson. He dreaded the idea of doing a presentation on a book in front of the other kids and hoped there might be a way out of it. He tried to concentrate on the first presentation by Connor about a Chris Ryan book. He made it seem easy, but Luke wasn't sure if that was because the book an easy subject to make interesting, or whether Connor was a confident presenter. When he had finished Sophie stood up and started talking about vampires. Luke's attention started to wander. He had so many things on his mind. He was worried about giving his presentation; his running and how long he could keep it secret from everyone; how long he could avoid the ABA; and his upcoming court case. He decided he should try and find Mr Strachan during the next break so that he could ask if he would be willing to attend court with him.

Luke was relieved to hear the bell ring before he was called up to give his presentation. He stuffed his books into his bag and was walking towards the staff room when he bumped into Scott.

'Hey guess what? Me and Robbie went to the art gallery on Saturday. You should have come, it was great.'

Over Scott's shoulder, Luke could see Mr Strachan coming out of the staff room and heading to the gym for his next lesson. He barely had time to register Scott's comments as he dashed after him.

'Sir, err, I've got my date for court.'

'Yes?'

'And I was wondering if there was any chance you could come with me, Sir.'

Mr Strachan was caught off-guard. 'I'm not sure.'

'I have already asked my mum and stepdad and Nan.'

'Well come back at lunchtime when I can check my timetable and we'll work something out.'

'Thanks, sir.'

That meant he would have to stay and attend his next lesson. If only he could remember what his next lesson on a Monday was. He searched through his pockets and bag and eventually found a battered copy of his timetable. As he wandered to his art lesson, he tried to remember what had originally possessed him to choose art as a GCSE option.

As he approached the art room, he noticed that all the other students had huge plastic folders with examples of their work. He had no equipment and no previous work. As he checked out the other kids to see if there was anyone he could borrow stuff from, he was staggered to spot Robbie. They stood and stared at one another for a moment, and then both spoke at once.

'What the hell are you doing here?'

Robbie replied 'Couldn't find you, and I had nothing else to do, so I came to class. Where have you been?'

Luke didn't want to admit he had been to English but explained that he had come to ask Mr Strachan to attend court with him and had to wait until after this lesson. He then noticed that Robbie had one of the large folders that the other pupils had.

'What's that? How long have you been coming to art classes?'

'Not long.'

'Well let me see your work then.'

'No.'

'Go on. I'm not going to laugh.'

'No, get stuffed.'

Mr Brown the art teacher unlocked the classroom and told the pupils to enter. On two of the walls, there were large prints of murals produced by Ford Madox Brown, who Mr Brown was allegedly named after. He spotted Luke and asked what he was doing there.

'I'm in this class, sir.'

'I don't recall ever seeing you before. Where are your materials?'

He glanced at Robbie for help, but Robbie just shrugged and stepped away.

'I haven't got any sir. I wasn't sure what I needed.'

'Everyone was given a comprehensive list when they arrived at the beginning of last term. Where were you at the beginning of *last* term?'

Luke couldn't think of a plausible answer and was already regretting coming to class.

'Well?'

'Sorry, sir.'

'Right. Sit over there.' He pointed to a desk on the opposite side of the room to Robbie's. He then proceeded to arrange a wine bottle and some fruit on a table in the middle of the room.

'You can either draw this with a 2B pencil or use charcoal. I want to see your work at the end of the lesson.'

Luke was given some paper and a piece of charcoal. He tried to use the charcoal but gave up and taking a pencil out of his pocket began to sketch the still life. He glanced up occasionally in an attempt to catch Robbie's eye, but Robbie seemed to be avoiding his stare. At the end of the lesson, Mr Brown went around the class peering over the shoulders of the pupils. He made various comments such as 'not bad' and 'what the bloody hell is that supposed to be?' When he got to Robbie he merely snorted. Robbie looked deflated, as he appeared to be expecting some praise. He passed by a couple of pupils with barely a glance but when he got to Luke he paused.

'That's good boy. You have a fine eye for detail and perspective. What's your name again?'

'Luke, sir.'

'Well Luke, here is your list of materials. Make sure you bring them to the next lesson.'

As everyone started packing up to leave, he reminded them that their homework for the following week was a self-portrait.

As Robbie sauntered over, Luke said, 'I'm definitely never coming to another art class.'

'Why not? He thinks you've got a *fine eye for detail*.' He said mimicking Mr Brown's lofty tones. 'Let's see it.'

'No.'

'Come on.'

'No. You show me yours and I'll show you mine.'

They both laughed as they walked out of the classroom.

'By the way, Scott told me you went to the art exhibition together.'

'Scott wanted to go, and mum bought me some trainers for taking him.'

Luke wished he could believe him.

Chapter 14 – In the Village – Social Media

After the meeting, Joey talked about setting up the Doodle poll on the computer and getting everyone to respond with their availability for the next meeting.

'I don't think that will work Joey. How many people around here even have a computer or know what a Doodle poll is?'

'Quite a few of them, probably. Do you realise Dad that it's your generation that knows next to nothing about technology? Older people are using it because it gives people who are isolated an opportunity to contact their family and friends, even if they're housebound.'

'What do you mean, my generation?'

'Seriously dad. When I was in the library the other week, Catherine's mum was in there and she said that she had heard about someone who had contacted old friends through the internet. I suggested she try Google images if she knew what the person looked like.'

'Really? I wonder who she's trying to find?'

'She's trying to contact her other daughter, Genevieve.'

'I didn't know she had another daughter,' said James.

'Neither did I until she mentioned her,' said Joey.

'Oh yes. She was a bit of a handful. She left home when she was about sixteen,' said Paul.

'Why?' Chorused James and Joey.

'I seem to remember she wanted to go on a school trip to London and her parents couldn't afford it.'

'So, she couldn't go?' asked James

'Oh, she went alright. When everyone came back and started talking about how wonderful everything was in the big city it made her furious. So, she packed a bag and stole some money from the till in the café.'

'And what happened?' asked James.

'She sent them a postcard from London saying she was squatting in a dirty old flat and she was frightened. She gave them the address and everything.'

'And what did they do?' Asked Joey.

'They got someone to take care of Catherine, who was only young at the time, and went all the way to London. I don't think either of them left the village before or after that.'

'Did they find her?' They both wanted to know.

'Yes, she was waiting outside as bold as brass. She'd actually been staying in a B & B.'

'Why did she do all that? Was it just for attention?' James wanted to know.

'Well she thought they would be so pleased to see her safe and well they would take her to all the sites of London to show her how much she meant to them.'

'And did they?' Queried Joey.

'No. They were so furious and upset they turned and walked away back towards the train station. She came back home with them as meek as you like, but it didn't last long. She was soon stealing bottles of vodka from the shop and getting drunk. She was hardly in a fit state to go to school some days. In fact, one day she didn't stay in school and Catherine had to find her own way home. I think she was only six or seven at the time.'

'No wonder they never talk about her,' stated James.

'Exactly. Anyway, I think village life was just too quiet for the likes of Genevieve and she left home for good. I'm not sure if they've heard from her since,' said Paul.

'Well I said to Sally that I thought if Google didn't work, Facebook might be a better option, so I showed her how to create a profile for herself, and then how to search for Genevieve Jones,' said Joey.

'Did she find her?' Paul and James asked at the same time.

'Yes, and she made a friend request.'

'Did Genevieve accept it?' Asked James.

'I don't know. I didn't want to wait to find out in case it didn't go well.'

'Joey! You should have stayed and found out. You'll have to find a way to ask her,' said James.

'I can't just go up to her and ask her. Don't be nosy.'

'Yes, James. Don't be nosy,' said Paul.

'Oh, as if you aren't dying to know,' replied James.

'Exactly. So, you should find a way to subtly ask her Joey,' said Paul.

'I'm not sure asking Joey to do anything subtly is a good idea,' remarked James.

'I can be subtle when I need to be. Anyway, I don't need to ask her. When I logged in with dad's account I set her profile up, and I added myself as a friend. So, I can go and check the threads of her conversations and see if she has managed to add Genevieve as a friend. Just call me a genius.'

'That's really nosy. That's like spying. That's worse than just asking,' stated James.

'There's no pleasing you two. Anyway living in this village, you can't keep a secret for long.'

'I know. Remember the time when you wet your pants in church and everyone was laughing about it for days,' reminded James.

Joey was mortified that James had brought this up so responded with, 'And remember when you sent that hand-made Valentine's day card to Anna Jones in your class and it went to Mrs Jones at the doctor's surgery? Her husband was so angry it caused a huge row and you had to own up.'

'That's the problem in a village where there aren't enough surnames to go around. There was a time when we had a Welsh rugby team and ten of the players had the surname, Jones.'

'So they all had weird nicknames such as Jones the Bones because he was a butcher, and Jones Loans the banker,' added James.

'Exactly. Okay, Joey. You email as many people as you can and for anyone you haven't got an email address, try and friend them on Facebook. Everyone else we'll ring round.'

'Thinking about it though, that still might not be enough people to stop the development.'

'Well, what else can we do?'

'I don't know but we have to try everything we can. Otherwise, this will change our lives forever.'

'Don't be so dramatic, Dad. It will only be a few houses.'

'It will still change everything. Remember what it was like when Fred moved into the farm next door? Everybody had something to say about him and his strange ideas.'

'That's because he was a townie and didn't know anything about farming.'

'Well, everyone who moves in could be the same. Just imagine sixty families like Fred.'

'Oh no, that's a grim thought,' agreed James.

'William told me that Fred is planning to do the cross-country race. Can you imagine Fred in a pair of shorts?' Asked Paul.

'No, and I don't want to imagine it. Why would he want to do the race? He's completely unfit.' Replied Joey.

'Apparently, he's got a bit of a soft spot for Catherine and he thinks it might be a way to impress her and get into shape at the same time.'

'Shouldn't he get into shape before he tackles something like that?' Asked James.

'I'm just warning you because you might see him running the course in the next few weeks,' informed Paul.

'Maybe when he finds out how harsh it is he'll realise his limitations,' said Joey.

'Well, I hope he doesn't get in the way. With the speeds you two have been achieving recently, you stand a good chance of not completely humiliating me.'

James and Joey exchanged glances but didn't pass a remark.

Joey had skyped, doodled and called everyone he could think of regarding the development. He wished there was an easier way to communicate with everyone and from the responses he'd had so far he noted that there was still huge opposition to it. He had taken the opportunity to check to see if Genevieve Jones had accepted Sally's friend invitation on Facebook.

The day before the meeting William had popped over to show them a letter he had received from a local councillor who was in the opposition party. It was printed on thick cream paper and had the portcullis crest of the House of Commons on the top of it. The councillor, Owen Deverill, said that he supported their plans to block the building of the new houses.

'So, what does this mean exactly?' Paul wanted to know.

'Well, it means that Deverill will speak up for us at the next council meeting. However, there are about twenty councillors who all get a vote each. But he has promised he will try and drum up some support from the other councillors beforehand.'

'That's fantastic news. I just can't understand Reg's desire to have it here,' said James.

'I can. Mr Martin showed me a letter on the internet which said there was some kind of benefit for councils who built more houses,' said Joey.

'What? Why didn't you mention that before?' asked Paul. William just stood with his mouth open.

'Sorry, I forgot to mention it.'

'What kind of benefits do they receive then?' queried William.

'I don't know, it just said they would receive "powerful incentives" to build new houses.'

'Oh, for God's sake. We don't stand a chance. I bet Reg will be lining his pockets already,' said William.

'Well let's not give up without a fight. Can you show us the letter, Joey?' Asked Paul.

'Yes, I printed it off to show you, I can't remember why I didn't give it to you.'

James suddenly recalled the occasion when Joey had come home with some news and he had asked him to just forget about it for the night. He was about to accept responsibility when his Dad and William finished reading the letter. They were obviously furious, and his courage deserted him. They were quoting phrases from the letter from The Communities Secretary which said *"I can confirm that this will ensure those local authorities that take action now to support the construction of new homes will receive substantial benefit for their actions. We are committed to housing growth and these incentives will be a priority."*

William resorted to speaking in Welsh, which he often did when he was upset. He seemed to be mainly talking to himself. As his anger abated, he sat down on one of the chairs in the kitchen and looked utterly defeated.

'William, I think we should still have the meeting tomorrow. There may be something we can do,' said Paul.

'What's the point? We've been told it's not an Area of Outstanding Natural Beauty. More than half of the people in the village seem to like the idea. And now this... Reg has won, hasn't he?'

'*Daliwch ati*, don't give up. Let's not make it easy for him.'

After some discussion on the matter, they decided to still attend the meeting. The doodle poll had revealed that at least twenty people would attend. They would meet at the Jones' and squash into the living room the following afternoon.

It was pouring with rain when they woke on Saturday morning. Joey and James were going to run the entire cross-country course again. The last time they had run it, Huw Morgan and his son Lloyd were running the last section, over and over again, which seemed a bit pointless, as it was by far the easiest stretch of the route. When Lloyd got to the finishing post he insisted on doing some noisy whoop-whoops and high-fives with his dad. As James and Joey passed them, they made some disparaging remarks about the state of Joey's running gear. Joey wasn't usually particularly aware of his appearance, but he suddenly felt self-conscious. He seemed to have the same dream night after night now, of James beating Lloyd Morgan. He had to. It didn't matter if he didn't win the race, but he needed to beat that smug swine, Morgan. He repeated to himself '*dal ati*', keep at it.

When everyone was sitting or standing comfortably, William brought everyone up to date with the report from the surveyor.

'Basically, he said that it isn't an Area of Outstanding Natural Beauty or a Site of Nature Conservation Importance. I did ask if there was any way to make it comply, but he didn't think any of them would apply here.'

'Such as?' asked Rhodri.

'Well in some areas people have moved rare newts or bats, which are both protected species, into an area so that it couldn't be interfered with.'

'And since there are no major trees or buildings that could house bats, or rivers for the newts, we couldn't do that?' said Rhodri.

'Exactly. I sent a petition to everyone in the area and presented it to Owen Deverill. He agreed to vote against the plans at the next council meeting.'

Paul interjected at this point. He passed around copies of the letter from the Communities Secretary. There were gasps and several expletives muttered as everyone read the letter. They were quoting particular phrases such as "powerful incentives so that people see the benefits of building", and "those who support the construction of new homes will receive direct and substantial benefit for their actions." Everyone started talking and arguing at the same time, so Paul called the meeting to order.

'Listen, we just have to attend the next council meeting and make sure that Deverill votes exactly as he promised.'

'But even with his support, will that be enough to sway the rest of the council?' asked Rhodri.

'I don't know. There can't be many people on the council in this area though can there? We need to find out who they are and get them on our side as quickly as possible.'

'Righto, I'll find out who they all are and start ringing them all. I'll email you all as soon as I've spoken to every one of them,' stated Rhodri.

Chapter 15 – In the City – The Taxi

Luke had finished his presentation for his English lesson and surprised himself and her by asking his mum if he could read it to her. She was watching her favourite soap on television and one of the main characters was about to get his comeuppance, but as Luke had never done any homework to her knowledge, let alone asked for her opinion, she decided to switch the television off and give him her undivided attention. He was getting to the part where he was explaining how Mo Farah moved from running out of necessity to considering running professionally when Damian came back into the room.

'What's going on?' demanded Damian.

'Luke's just telling me about his presentation for English.'

'Sounds boring. We're not missing Corrie for that crap.'

'It's only five minutes love.'

'Well, it can wait then can't it?'

'Let's go to the kitchen, you can tell me the rest of it.'

'No, it doesn't matter.'

As he slammed out he waited to see if his mum would follow him. She didn't. He heard her ask Damian why he couldn't just give Luke a little bit of attention. He didn't want to eavesdrop on the rest of the conversation but he couldn't drag himself away.

'Because I've got more important things on my mind, that's why.'

'Such as?'

'Such as the fact that the police came round to the taxi office today. They caught me putting red diesel into one of the cabs.'

'Well you've paid for it, why shouldn't you use it?'

'Because it's only intended for vehicles that don't use the road.'

'What kind of vehicle would you have that you wouldn't want to use on a road?'

'Bloody tractors, cranes and the like.'

'Well, why did you put it in the taxi then?'

'Because it's a fraction of the price, of course, you silly bitch. And now the police have seized the taxi and it wasn't even mine, and it'll probably be crushed.'

'Oh no! How will you pay for it?'

'Well, I have been thinking about changing jobs for a while anyway.'

'How long would it be before you earned enough to pay for the car?'

'I wouldn't pay for it. I'd just do a runner.'

'Do a runner? What kind of example would that be to Luke?'

'Why don't you stop mollycoddling that lad and join the real world?'

'I don't mollycoddle him. I don't spend enough time with him.'

'Course you do. You're here every morning and night.'

'Just long enough to make sure he gets breakfast and dinner.'

'So what? Anyway, Andrew reckons he could get me another job quite easily.'

'Who's Andrew?'

'Robbie's dad. He was in the pub last night and said he's going to start running a new building site just inside Wales and they need skilled men.'

'I'm not being funny but what skills have you got?'

'I am a bricklayer! I was a brickie before I worked at the taxi office. I was bloody good too.'

'Oh really?'

'Yeah really. No need to sound so surprised. Forget Corrie, I'm going to the pub.'

Luke quickly dashed to his bedroom. After he heard Damian leave he went to speak to his mum.

'Damian's thinking of leaving his job at the taxi office and going to work on a building site in Wales.'

'I know. I heard.'

'I'm really worried. What if he leaves us?'

'So what? I hope he does leave.'

'Don't be silly. We couldn't afford this mortgage without both our salaries.'

'I thought this was a council flat.'

'It was. But I bought it about ten years ago. The mortgage is less than the rent so it's a good investment.'

'But it's a dump.'

'Well, I'm sorry you feel like that. But property doesn't come cheap in Manchester. If I didn't work such long hours at the factory, we wouldn't be able to afford it.'

Luke had popped into the sausage factory once when she was at work and there were huge vats with odd-shaped bits and pieces swirling around in them. His mum had told him that every single piece of the pig was used, but he preferred to convince himself that she was joking. The raw meat then went through several processes until it was an even pink mush. This was then fed through a machine with a long tube on the end of it. The skin of the sausage was then held in place by a type of calliper as the meaty mush was pumped into it. This caused lots of ribald comments among the workforce. The amount of salt in the skins affected the complexions of the staff and most had lots of small cuts and spots as a result of working there.

Even though he wasn't particularly ambitious, he didn't want to go and work at the sausage factory with his mum and her mates.

Luke decided to go round to Robbie's to find out more about his visit to the art gallery, then hopefully have enough time for a run before going home. On the way he saw the ABA skulking near the back of The Old Crow, so he ducked into the newsagents. He had the money his Nan had given him for cleaning the caravan, but he didn't want to spend it on rubbish. He peered between the notices in the window, but the gang were loitering on the opposite side of the road. He decided to read through the magazines and picked up the first one that came to hand. As he opened it up there was a full-page picture of a man in shorts, with an impressive six-pack. He wasn't immediately sure what kind of magazine it was but as he read the title he realised it was a running magazine. It offered nutrition advice, running routes and groups. He didn't know whether to take it or not and as the newsagent was getting a bit huffy he had to hurry up and make a decision.

'This isn't a library you know.'

'I'll take this.'

He took the magazine and checked to see if the ABA had moved on. There was no sign of them so he left the shop and ran over to Robbie's. He knocked on the door and Robbie's mum Sandra answered, wearing her trademark tracksuit. She was usually surly towards Luke but she greeted him warmly. 'Thanks for coming over. I know Scott will appreciate it.'

Luke couldn't remember a time when she had last been pleasant to him, but he knew it had to be several years at least. He went through to Robbie and Scott's bedroom and was horrified at what he saw. Scott had been badly beaten. His left eye was completely closed, surrounded by a huge purple swelling. His lip was split where his teeth had gone through it and there was blood crusted around his nose. He dropped the magazine on the bed and went over to Scott.

'What happened?'

'The ABA. They said they had seen him hanging around the graffiti and they were convinced he was responsible for all the recent changes.'

'But you haven't been hanging around it.'

'I did write down that pirate word, and I put it on a group WhatsApp chat.'

'But what does that prove?'

'They said because I knew what it meant it must have been me.'

'But anyone could have worked that out.'

'They booted my bag and heard the spray can as it hit the floor.'

'Spray can? You idiot, what were you doing with a spray can in your bag?

As usual, whenever Scott felt awkward and had said enough, he hung his head. Luke couldn't get any more out of him but believed him completely when he said he hadn't done any damage to the graffiti. He couldn't help wondering if Robbie had literally got him to carry the can for him, and if so did that mean he was responsible for all the blue man artwork?

'Well, what are we going to do now?' Luke asked Robbie.

'What can we do? Even with our whole gang we probably couldn't take any one of the ABA.'

Luke knew it to be true and had never felt so powerless in his life.

Robbie noticed the magazine and picked it up.

He read one of the headlines on the cover: 'Men's running tights, *to provide moisture management and excellent freedom of movement?* What the hell?'

'I went into Tommy's newsagents to avoid the ABA and I had to buy something.'

'What was wrong with a Mars bar?' asked Robbie.

'Or a Bounty?' asked Scott.

'Or a Twix?' asked Robbie.

'Or a Crunchie? asked Scott.

He knew they could keep this up all night so in the end, he decided to come clean.

'Okay, I've started running. I've been meaning to tell you.'

'Running? Why for God's sake?'

'What's wrong with running?'

'It's boring, tiring, makes you sweaty, none of my friends do it.'

'I do it!'

'You're a wimp.'

'But I'm fit.'

'I'm fit.'

'No, you're not. You're always puffing and wheezing when we have to take the stairs.'

'That's because of my asthma.'

Luke decided to change the subject. 'At least it's not art.'

'There's nothing wrong with art, besides you came to the last art class.'

'So? I only went to that lesson because I had to hang around for Mr Strachan. Why did you go?'

'Because it's not bad. Mr Brown is alright, some of his lessons are quite interesting really.'

Scott, realising that Robbie made a poor case, produced the programme of the art exhibition they had attended. It was open at some of Banksy's work. There was a print of two children playing with a sign which read "No ball games" and one of a chimpanzee with a sign around its neck reading "Laugh now, but one day we'll be in charge." Luke thought they were quite interesting, but it would take a lot more than a few well-executed stencils to improve his impression of art.

He told Robbie and Scott about the conversation he had had with his mum. They couldn't imagine Damian working on a building site any more than Luke could.

Chapter 16 – In the Village – Joey's Letter

Joey was haphazardly vacuuming the living room when the phone rang. It was Rhodri. He asked Joey to pass a message on to his dad and everyone on the committee. He had contacted all the councillors in the area, and they had all either politely given him the brush off or been completely non-committal about supporting them. He assumed that Reg must have got to them all. He also mentioned that the next meeting of the council would take place the following Monday when the plans would be on the agenda.

It was after eight, and there was still no sign of their dad. They were feeling uneasy so James thought they should try and ring his mobile, as he may have broken down somewhere. It rang and rang. The weather was terrible, it was beginning to drizzle and it was fully dark. After what felt like an eternity the house phone rang. It was Paul.

'Sorry I'm late. The traffic on the motorway was terrible; then I got a puncture just outside Llugwy. It took me ages to change the tyre because it was so dark and there was no street lighting. But I'm on my way now.'

'Thank God dad. We've been really worried.'

'Sorry, you know what it's like trying to get a signal down in the valley, so I had to find a payphone. Put the kettle on, I'll be home as soon as I can.'

Joey had composed an email and sent it around to everyone, but James thought he ought to have let their dad check it first.

Dear Neighbours,

Sorry to give you all some dreadful news but it looks like all the councillors have been tampered with and now none of them will help us to get rid of Reg and his housing estate. If anyone can think of any last-minute tactics to get rid of this unwelcome building site, please let us know and we will support you.

We need to stick together.

This may be our last chance.

From the Joneses (Joey, James and Paul)

Chapter 17 – In the City – Damian's Job

'Damian has got the job on a building site in a new development in Wales. I don't want him to commute that far every day, you know he's not the best driver, and it's a great opportunity to keep you out of trouble. I've decided that we're going to move there.' Luke's mum told him as soon as he walked through the door of the flat.

'Why do we have to go too?' asked Luke.

'Because we're a family and we should stick together. This is a great opportunity for us to move to a house with a garden.'

'You don't know anything about gardening!'

'Well I can learn, and so can you. It will be a fresh start, and I don't want you to mention it to Robbie. I want us to just pack our bags and leave without a big fuss.'

'You mean do a runner? Why we haven't done anything wrong?' he pleaded.

'I'm sick of all the aggravation and the snide remarks from the neighbours. I want to get you away from Robbie. He's a bad influence, and as long as you're going around with him, you will always be getting into trouble.'

'Mum, he's not the one getting me into trouble. Why can't you understand?'

'How can I possibly understand? You steal cigarettes, time and time again, and you don't even smoke.'

'Will you just listen to me, Mum, please?'

'If you're going to start telling me another pack of lies, don't bother.'

'It's not lies; why are you so blind? You pick men who are complete losers or bullies and I'm the one who always suffers. And now I'm expected to lose all my friends and move to some boring dump in the middle of nowhere,' he shouted.

'Don't you dare speak to me like that. I'm your mother, and you'll treat me with respect while you're under my roof, lad!' she shouted back.

'I'm going out, and I'm not going to live in some hole miles from anywhere. You can go without me.' He grabbed his keys and slamming the door as loud as he could, he left.

He ran round to his Nan's house. When he got there, he found her changing the bedding in the caravan which was parked on her driveway.

'Hiya Nan. What are you doing? I could do that for you.'

'I know love, but I thought it might be needed quite soon so I decided I'd better make a start on tidying it up a bit.'

'Why will it be needed quite soon? You don't usually go to the caravan park until June.'

'Hasn't your mum told you?'

'Told me what?'

'Why don't we go inside and have a nice cup of tea?'

'I don't want tea. Told me what?'

'That you're going to live in the caravan on a building site in Wales.'

'This just gets better and better.'

'What do you mean?'

'Mum said we would be living in a house – with a garden!'

'Well, maybe you will eventually. But Damian has to build the house first.'

Luke felt like exploding but remained incredibly calm. 'Can you honestly imagine Damian building a house that would be fit to live in? Seriously?'

'Well, apparently he used to be a bricklayer. Maybe he'll surprise us all.'

'I doubt it!'

'I don't think you'll have much choice.'

'Couldn't I come and live here with you?'

'Sorry love. It's just not possible. I don't earn enough to feed a growing lad.'

Luke felt defeated. 'I wish I could win the marathon. Then I wouldn't need either of them.'

'I thought people had to pay to do the marathon.'

'They do. But there's prize money for the first three places at least. I've been reading about it in a magazine I got.'

'That sounds like a change from the usual magazines you read.'

'Nan!'

'I meant that you used to read comics when you were little.'

'It's been a long time since I read a comic. Actually, I've started reading a book in my English lesson, called "Twin Ambitions".'

'Really?'

'Yes, I'm doing a presentation on it this week at school. It's about Mo Farah. Did you know he came to England when he was eight and had to leave his twin in Somalia because he was too ill to travel? When his dad went back for him the family he was living with had moved. It was twelve years before they finally tracked him down.' His Nan was so surprised at this unusual turn of events, she let him talk through his presentation, to take his mind off moving to Rowan.

Chapter 18 – In the Village – The Vote

The council meeting was being held on a Monday evening at the Town Hall in Llugwy. There wasn't a separate one in Rowan as the village was too small to warrant its own Town Hall. The entrance hall to the building was quite spacious and had a beautiful black and white marble floor. To the right, there was a large fireplace with an ornate surround. There were several doors, all painted black, with colourful coats of arms above each one. They represented various dynasties such as Llewellyn the Great, Owain Edmond and the Kingdom of Gwynedd. They were made up of images of dragons, lions, fleur de Lys and eagles.

The chamber was full, including the public gallery. The meeting was called to order by the Chair, a gruff old man with mutton-chop whiskers and an old tweed jacket.

'*Nos dda*, good evening, ladies and gentlemen. We have only one item on the agenda, which is for the vote on the planning request for a small housing development at Rowan.'

Everybody in the chamber sat quietly, and there was an air of despondency to the proceedings. Joey and James were fidgeting nervously. The Chair went through the routine process of accepting the apologies of those members who couldn't make it, these included both Reg Russell and Owen Deverill.

Joey wanted to know why Reg and Deverill were apologising.

'They are apologising for their absence,' explained Paul.

'Pity they're not here in person to apologise for all the aggravation they've caused,' complained James.

The Chair then asked one of the representatives of Millers Homes to present the plans for the new houses. He stood and showed a large-scale map which detailed the village as it was, with a red-shaded area where the new houses would be built, if the plans were approved. The shaded area didn't appear substantial. It would easily have fitted into one of William's fields, which presumably meant that there would be just small gardens attached to each house. He then showed a more detailed plan of the area, which showed different-sized houses. They were to be a combination of two, three and four-bedroomed houses.

Joey fidgeted as The Chair explained there had been a demand for additional housing in the area for some time; that Miller Developments had an excellent track record of building houses in rural areas which were complementary to their surroundings; the additional residents would generate additional income in the area; and that the school and church would be secure. He acknowledged the various concerns and complaints from members of the public and hoped they would be reassured by the promises given by the Developers. Joey just wanted him to stop rambling and get to the vote.

'All those in favour please raise your hands.'

The secretary did a quick headcount and jotted a number down.

'All those opposed to the plans.'

The secretary duly noted something in her book.

'Any abstentions?'

There were none.

Everyone stood up to leave at the same time.

The following morning Joey went into the shop and was shocked to notice a poster on the noticeboard asking for applications for the following positions: Bricklayers, Electricians, Engineers, Plasterers, Scaffolders and Roofers. The vote had only been cast the previous evening. Everyone had barely had time to register their shock at what had happened, and now the developers were already asking the villagers to work for them.

He picked some items for his latest cookery class and took them to Catherine. She gave him his change and Joey asked her, 'how did they manage to get these posters made in such a short space of time when they couldn't possibly have known how the vote would go?'

'I've been wondering that myself,' she replied.

Joey hadn't seen Tommo for a while and the cannabis was playing on his mind, but right now he was more concerned about the notices asking for skilled workmen, which were dotted around the village. He decided to mention it to his Dad when he came home.

'Well they didn't waste any time, did they?'

'Dad, would you consider going to work for them? It would be a lot easier than working in Manchester.'

'I know it would, and there is nothing I would like more, but I just couldn't face the thought of it now.'

'But other people might, and they might only need a couple of electricians. What if all the jobs go quickly?'

'Joey I would love to work locally. The worst part of my day is travelling to and from Manchester, but can you imagine how William would take it? He would regard it as a complete betrayal.'

'Well has he said anything to you about working for them?'

'No, I haven't seen him since the vote, I think he's been avoiding everyone.'

Chapter 19 – In the City – The Magistrates' Court

Luke had hardly slept all night. He was furious with his mum and Damian and was still refusing to believe that they would actually have to move to a building site in Wales. He was also nervous about attending court and could hardly button his shirt up. He had taken care of his appearance today and was determined to try and give a good impression of himself. Unfortunately, he was all too aware that he had quite a few offences to his name, mainly for shoplifting, but also for grievous bodily harm, which he suspected the Magistrates would take into consideration.

Luke had arranged to meet Mr Strachan outside the court, fifteen minutes before he was due to be called. His mum had offered to take the day off work, but he said he would be fine. He suspected she was feeling a bit guilty about the way she had handled things. She still wasn't prepared to believe that he was only nicking the cigs for Damian, and he didn't know what to say to her, but he was happy that she'd made the offer.

The City of Salford Magistrates' court was on Wood Street and was a modern building with a long marble floor and glass and silver frontage. As he stood waiting for Mr Strachan, he could see the Sunset by Australasia Restaurant and the famous John Rylands library. He didn't know anyone who had been in either one of those places, but he was related to several people who had attended the courthouse.

He saw Mr Strachan approaching, and walked towards him, making sure his shirt was tucked in.

'Morning, Sir.'

'Morning, Luke. How are you feeling?'

'A bit nervous, sir. I didn't sleep properly last night.'

'Well try not to worry. They'll be able to tell that you're genuinely sorry. What is the name of the solicitor you've been appointed?'

'It's Mr Bagshaw, he said he would meet us inside in a couple of minutes.'

As Luke couldn't afford a solicitor, he had been allocated Mr Bagshaw who was the duty solicitor that day. He approached Luke and Mr Strachan, looking pretty harassed. His hair was floppy and untidy, and he was wearing a blue and white checked shirt, a navy-blue tie with a stain on it and a black polyester suit that had shiny patches on it.

He introduced himself to Luke and Mr Strachan and advised Luke to plead guilty, as there was just too much evidence against him. His was the first case to be heard, and he was told where to sit inside the courtroom. As it was a magistrates' court, there would be three magistrates as opposed to a judge and jury.

Luke squirmed as PC Jenkins stepped up to give evidence. He showed pictures of Luke and Robbie from the CCTV cameras in the bus station. He pointed out the rucksack that Luke had on his back, which he had used to put all the stolen items in; this proved that he had come prepared and that it wasn't just a spur-of-the-moment decision. He then explained what had happened – how

110

Robbie had caused a distraction with a fizzy drink so that Luke could help himself to the cigarettes.

The next person to give evidence was the shop assistant. She described what had happened and that she had given chase and caught the chubby lad (at which Luke hid a smirk) and that she had called for assistance using the walkie-talkie that most of the shops used to summon additional security. Whilst she was detaining Robbie, she had been unable to catch Luke, and he had got away with several hundred pounds worth of cigarettes. She had called out to someone to stop Luke, but he had managed to escape them and, in the process, had barged into a pram with a toddler in it, causing the child to be knocked to the ground. The child had attended the hospital for minor injuries. This made the chief magistrate frown disapprovingly in his direction.

The last person to give evidence was the mother of the injured baby. She described that she had been shopping with her husband and their daughter when the incident took place. She then went on to state that the shock had badly affected her, and she hadn't been able to return to work yet. The judge was quite sympathetic, and Luke felt a surge of shame. For some reason, he suddenly thought of his nan and how disappointed she would be.

Luke then went up onto the stand. He swore on the bible that he would tell the truth and then waited nervously while the prosecutor flicked through his notes for what seemed like an age. The prosecutor, whose name was Timothy Spencer, stood and asked Luke why he had stolen the goods. He said that it had been a prank that had got out of hand and that he was genuinely sorry. Mr Spencer said that was probably what he had said last time, at which point the duty solicitor stood and objected to the allusion to incidents that may or may not have occurred in the past. The chief magistrate said, 'Sustained; please stick to the facts of this incident, Mr Spencer.'

The prosecutor then started asking awkward questions and tried to make Luke seem like a liar. He asked, 'How good a friend would you say that you are?' and Luke replied, 'A good friend.'

'Really?' sneered Mr Spencer. 'Isn't it true that you stole all of the goods then ran away and left your less-fit friend to face the music?'

Luke couldn't think of anything to say to that.

After several more minutes of questions, Mr Spencer couldn't trip him up or ask him any more awkward questions, so he said, 'I have nothing further, Your Honours.'

The magistrates retired to their chambers to consider all of the evidence. When they returned, the usher said, 'All rise,' and everyone stood up briefly. He asked Luke to remain standing.

The chief magistrate then made his pronouncement, 'Luke Mills, for the offence of shoplifting, after careful consideration, we find you guilty and have decided to give you a community service order of one hundred hours and a fine of one hundred and twenty pounds which will be paid as compensation to the newsagents. Regarding the matter of the injury to the child, we are of the mind that you panicked and accidentally struck out. Therefore we find you not guilty.'

As he prepared to leave the court he felt as if a huge weight had been lifted from his shoulders. He thanked Mr Strachan and Mr Bagshaw. Mr Strachan offered him a lift back to school, but as it was only a five-minute walk away and he wanted to let his mum know what had happened, he declined.

He texted his mum to give her the news and told her he was on his way past the sausage factory. He hoped that the good news might encourage her to stay in Manchester. She briefly popped outside and hugged him.

'I'm so relieved for you, love.'

'Me too.'

'We need to sit down and talk properly tonight, and you can show me your presentation if you like.'

'It doesn't matter. I've got to give it this afternoon. I'd better get to school; I've got science next.'

'Really? I thought you only got that excited about PE.'

'I've changed. Since speaking to Mr Strachan in the last month or so I've been paying attention, doing my homework and stuff. I went to a science lesson last week and this week we're doing something with a van der Graaf generator.'

'What possessed you to go to a science class?'

'I go to all my classes now, except for art. God knows why I picked that.'

'Probably because it was an easy subject to skive off from.'

'Maybe.'

'Well get off to school and we'll talk properly when I get home.'

Luke made it in time for the start of his science lesson. The teacher had placed the van der Graaf generator in the middle of his desk and asked all the pupils to stand in a circle around the room, holding hands. Then he chose Abigail, the girl with the longest hair in the class, to place her hands on the large silver globe. He switched the generator on, and her hair stood on end. Then he switched it off and asked her to hold hands with the two pupils on either side of her, to form a large circle. The hair of one or two of the children on either side of her also stood up on their heads, and when someone was told to break the circle by letting go of their hands, they got a mild electric shock. They had to write up the details of the experiment and finish it off for homework.

Luke met Robbie during the break and told him what had happened at court.

'What type of stuff will you have to do for your Community Service?'

'Cleaning up graffiti.'

'Shit.'

'I know. I wonder if they'll let me do it somewhere else?'

'Maybe.' Robbie offered unconvincingly.

'I hope so.'

'Well, I hope you're not expecting me to pay towards the fine.'

'Of course I'm not. I've borrowed some from my Nan, but I've got to do jobs to pay it back.'

'Well tell her you don't want to. She can't make you.'

'She's my Nan.'

'Exactly. They're always a pushover.'

'I'm going to English. See you later.'

'Good luck with your presentation. Hope you make a balls of it.'

Luke had rehearsed his presentation at least a dozen times, and each time it sounded more practised and less interesting. He had found the book fascinating and tried to inject some of his own enthusiasm for running into it, but unless the other kids in the class liked running, he couldn't imagine them listening for more than thirty seconds.

Miss Littleton could see he was nervous so decided that Luke should do his presentation first and get it over and done with.   He had chosen to do a PowerPoint presentation and opened with a brief video of Mo Farah winning a gold medal at the London Olympics for the 10,000m event, something he dreamt of for himself. He talked of Farah's description of his upbringing in Somalia where his twin Hassan still lived. They were separated at eight years old, when Mo, his two younger brothers, and his mother joined their father, who had been working and studying in the UK. Hassan was unwell and unable to travel, so stayed behind with family. When his father returned to collect Hassan, the family he was living with had moved and could not be found. He talked of his participation in English cross country runs from the age of 13, winning gold medals in the Olympics, and his success in World Championships. He then went on to talk about his success as a writer and finished by talking about some of his philanthropic work in Somalia. Luke couldn't help but be impressed and had to curb his enthusiasm a bit. When he finished no one spoke, and Luke was convinced he had bored them all to tears. But Miss Littleton broke the silence and asked if anyone had any questions. Everyone put their hands up and started asking questions at the same time. It seemed that when it came to charisma it would be a photo finish between Luke and Mo Farah.

Luke went home in a great mood. Even the thought of the community service couldn't upset his frame of mind.

He decided to make tea for himself and his mum, as Damian had gone to the pub. He took the pizzas out of the freezer and put them into the oven. When his mum came home, everything was nearly ready.

'Thanks love. Damian has popped to the pub for a drink to meet Robbie's dad. He's going to tell him a bit more about his new job in Wales.'

'Mum, I don't want to go. Can't I get a Saturday job and help out with the mortgage?'

'No, it needs a full-time wage. Just come to the village and you'll see, it's a lovely place. It's like Anglesey and some of the places we've been to on holiday.'

'I don't want to go. I want to stay here and go to school.'

'You hardly ever go to school. So, you can hardly ever go to school in Wales.'

'I go to all my classes now, I told you earlier.'

'I didn't believe you. Anyway, you can just transfer to the school in Llugwy.'

'Where?'

'Llugwy. Rowan hasn't got its own school, so you'll have to go to the one in the next town.'

'How small is it?'

'Well, it's big enough.'

'I've never even heard of the place, so it can't be that big.'

'You are coming with us. I will straighten you out for your own good before you end up like your worthless father.'

'But I'm going to school, doing my homework and even enjoying running through the streets round here.'

'I'm glad that you're growing up a bit and thinking about your future. But you were lucky this time that you only got community service. Once you start going to Young Offender's Institutes, it's a slippery slope.'

'That's what you think,' he shouted as he stood up and stormed out without finishing his pizza.

He ran down the road and past the Old Crow and his school. He kept going and decided to run towards the city, where it was well-lit. He liked being outside, and he was surprised at how running made him feel relaxed and free. He still hadn't spoken to his mum about it, and now he probably wouldn't be able to do the Manchester half marathon. Just as he thought life wasn't too bad, Damian had managed to ruin everything again.

As he dodged the traffic; several pedestrians; a lorry parked across the pavement and waited for some traffic lights to change, he remembered reading an article in the magazine about a cross-country race where they ran over hills and fields, through streams and under trees. It sounded a bit like Farah's early journey to school.

Chapter 20 –In the City - Community Service

Luke was wondering how his meeting with his Personal Placement Officer would go. They would be discussing his community service order. His mum, Beth, was going along with him to the office in the city centre. She explained to Mr Deacon that they would be moving into a caravan on the building site in the next week or so. They had discussed the various types of work that would be available to him, if it was being carried out in Manchester but decided that as he would be moving shortly they should find out more about what he could do in Rowan.

Mr Deacon rang the head of the village council in Rowan to see if they would have any work that would be suitable for Luke to do.

Luke could only hear Mr Deacon's end of the conversation, but apparently, he was speaking to someone called Reg who sounded as if he was being awkward. After a few minutes, Mr Deacon must have got the measure of Reg and said, 'Well, don't worry, if you haven't got anything, I will contact the next town to you instead.' Luke smirked as he could hear Reg backtracking rapidly.

After he replaced the 'phone, Mr Deacon told Luke that he would probably be reporting to a local farmer named William Llewellyn.

'If we don't end up going to Rowan, could I do the Community Service here instead?'

'I'm sure that could be arranged.'

'Don't bother,' said Beth.

'There are probably more options here, such as cleaning up graffiti and the like.'

At this Luke blanched.

'No, thank you. We're going to Rowan,' his mum said firmly.

'Well if you're sure.'

'We're sure.'

Mr Deacon shook their hands and showed them out.

As they left his office, Beth said through gritted teeth, 'we are going and that's the end of the matter.'

Luke had avoided Robbie so that he could go for a run around the city as he wasn't sure he would get many more opportunities to do so again, even though he was hoping that he could somehow convince his mum to stay in Manchester. It was dark as Luke neared the back entrance to his flat. He spotted Robbie crouched in a corner.

'What's happened?' asked Luke.

'I had a row with my mum. She kept babbling on about my dad's new job and moving house, so I stormed out.'

'What's wrong with moving house? Wouldn't you rather live in a house than a flat?'

'It's not round here. It's miles away in the middle of nowhere.'

As he stood up, Luke could see that Robbie was covered head to foot with blue spray paint. It was in his hair; all over his face; his clothes and even his trainers. Although he was horrified at what he saw, Luke had to suppress an urge to laugh. Robbie reminded him of Poppa Smurf.

'But who did this to you?'

'When I ran around the corner I bumped into Spud. I wasn't going to do anything to his pathetic mural, but he wouldn't believe me.'

Luke could hardly speak. He just stared at Robbie. He couldn't remember an occasion when he had seen Robbie crying, but he was sobbing and rubbing his eyes.

'Did he hurt you?'

'Yes.'

'What did he do?'

'I don't want to talk about it.'

'Do you want me to walk back home with you?'

'No!'

'I just meant in case the ABA were hanging about.'

'They can't do anything worse to me than Spud has done.'

'Please. Just tell me what's happened.'

'No, I can't. It was vile.'

'Oh, God. You should talk to someone.'

'Never! Anyway, my mum wanted me to keep it quiet, but I think you should know. We'll be moving house soon. So I probably won't see you again.'

'What? Where?'

'Somewhere I won't have to worry about bumping into the ABA. I've got to go. Don't come round, I've got to start packing. See you.'

Luke had been worrying about moving to Wales and how Robbie would handle it, but if he was moving because of his dad's new job then they must surely both be going to Wales.

Chapter 21 – in the Village - Application

Joey had decided to pop into the village on the way home from school so that he could read one of the notices again. He took out one of his exercise books and wrote the details on the back of it. Just as he was writing down the address to send applications to, Rhodri came up behind him. Rhodri was well over six feet tall and incredibly broad, so blotted out a lot of the light. Joey turned and looked up at him.

'You're a bit young to be applying for jobs aren't you, boyo?

'It's not for me.'

'Is it for your dad?'

'No.'

'James?'

'No.'

'Who then boyo?'

Joey squirmed like a fish on a hook. 'I know you were opposed to the building work, but would you not consider working there?'

'Actually, I'm thinking of applying. I was a bit worried about how everyone would feel about it, particularly your dad, but at the end of the day I've got to earn a living.'

'Well dad would like to work there but he's worried about you and William.'

'Tell him I haven't got a problem with it. But I think William is going to be a different kettle of fish.'

'Would you go and talk to William with dad, if he wanted you to?'

'I don't think he needs me to hold his hand. See you later Joey.'

Whilst he was in the café Catherine came over to him.

'I wanted to thank you for helping mum set up a Facebook page. That was helpful, that was.'

'I hope it helped.'

'So do I.'

Joey decided he couldn't really dig any further.

'Have you ever considered turning this into an internet café?'

'I've no idea what that means. What would it entail? I wouldn't want to put off my regular customers.'

'You could just have a couple of computers over in the corner and offer free Wi-Fi. I'm sure it would be really popular.'

'But most young people have got their own computers now, haven't they?'

'Yes, but it would be useful for people of your generation. Sorry, I didn't mean old people. Because you're not old, not really.'

Catherine raised an eyebrow and said, 'alright Joey, I think you should leave it there before you do some permanent damage.' She walked away laughing and shaking her head, as Joey skulked out, mortified with himself.

He hung up his coat and wandered into the kitchen where his dad and James were having a cup of tea.

'You two haven't done any training for a couple of days. If you want to have any hope of being anywhere near as good as me, you need to keep it up.'

Joey and James jumped up and had a mock fight with their dad which involved a lot of shouting but not much contact. After a couple of minutes, he surrendered.

'We'll go for a run after dinner. In the meantime, dad, have you had any more thoughts about working on the development?' Asked Joey

'It would be convenient but I'm not sure it would be worth losing all our friends over it.'

'I was speaking to Rhodri and he's decided to apply.'

'Did you say anything about me?'

'I said you were concerned about him and William.'

'I wonder if he'd come and chat to William with me.'

'Dad, you don't need Rhodri to hold your hand, do you?'

'No, I suppose not. I think I'll go to the pub after dinner and see if I can soften him up with a couple of tots of Penderyn Whisky.'

'What if he's not happy about the idea?'

'At the end of the day, I have to make my own mind up. I have to decide what's best for us.'

Whilst he was gone the boys got busy. James showed Joey an article online which said that if you mixed vinegar with washing-up liquid it helped it to stick to the crop. They found an old container in the garden shed and poured one of the bottles of vinegar into it, then a big squirt of washing-up liquid. They hid it at the back of the shed and then went and started doing their homework.

When Paul returned from the pub, he was somewhat the worse for wear. James and Joey were still up but were just getting ready to go to bed.

'Dad, how many have you had?'

'Just a couple.'

'A couple of drinks wouldn't get you in this state. What happened? Did you speak to William?'

'Yes, and I'll tell you all about it in the morning.'

'Dad, tell us now, or we won't be able to sleep.'

'Well, I bought him a couple of whiskies.'

'Yes.'

'And then Rhodri mentioned his friends who are serving in the army so we thought we would raise a glass of beer to them.'

'Yes.'

'And there were a couple of Americans in the pub and it seemed like a good idea to try one or two bourbons, just to be friendly.'

'And?'

'And Gavin said he had some relatives in Ireland, so we toasted them with an Irish whiskey.'

'No.'

'Then we had to have a nightcap, so we had a brandy each. It was the American's round so we said we always finish the night on a nice Cognac.'

'Oh no.'

'Oh yes. Fifteen pounds a shot.'

'What were you thinking?'

'Thinking? Boyo I haven't been able to think since shortly after nine tonight.'

'Oh, dad. Can you remember what you said to William?'

'It was probably, "let's have one for the road".'

'I meant about the job.'

'Oh yes, he seemed fine about it.'

'Fine? Are you sure?'

'I think so, but then he probably couldn't tell you much about the conversation either, but he was in a grand mood.'

'I wonder if he'll still be in a grand mood in the morning.'

Chapter 22 – In the Village – The Hangover

Paul had compiled his curriculum vitae and covering letter for the position of Senior Electrician on Joey's laptop. He asked James to check it over and then email it for him. When Joey popped into the corner shop for some Irn Bru for his dad, he remembered that he still had to buy more vinegar. If Catherine mentioned anything about the amount he was buying he would say that he accidentally smashed the last bottle.

Catherine asked how his dad was feeling.

'Well, he was a bit sulky.'

'Sulky?'

'Yes, quiet and grumpy.'

'That's a hangover for you. That must be why he needs the Irn Bru.'

'So, you were in the pub last night?'

'Yes, so was half the village.'

'Did you overhear his conversation with William?'

'They had lots of conversations. To be honest they weren't making much sense after they started hitting the hard stuff.'

'Did Dad mention he was going to apply for a job on the building site?'

'I don't know. Is he?'

'He wants to.'

'I'm not sure, they were getting a bit rowdy. They hustled some Americans on the pool table. Then played some drinking games.'

'So they were getting along really well?'

'Yes, but William will be like a bear with a sore head this morning and when he hears that your dad is going to apply for one of the jobs, he may react angrily.'

Joey decided to quickly change the subject.

'Has your mum heard from Genevieve yet?'

'Yes.' Then she turned away to serve another customer.

Luke felt dejected. He did not want to go to the village, but he didn't want to stay where he was. His teachers had separated him from Robbie for many of their lessons from the beginning of term and although he did have other friends, he didn't spend much time with them. If Robbie and Scott left and he had to perpetually avoid the ABA, his life would be grim.

He couldn't help wondering what had happened to Robbie. Whenever he so much as got a paper cut, he whinged about it, but now he was withdrawn and quiet. Robbie hadn't called, texted or liked anything on TikTok or Insta for days.

As he left the flats to go to school, he noticed that someone had written over the mural in huge blue letters, 'I'll get you back!'

As Luke thought about the events of recent weeks, he realised that Robbie must be going to the same village if Damian was going to be working for Robbie's dad. He composed a text to his mum.

'OK, I'll go 2 wales.'

'Thought we'd already agreed.'

'U mite of.'

Luke had tried to get hold of Robbie and Scott for a couple of days, but he kept getting the unavailable message. Although he and Robbie weren't together for many lessons, they always spent their breaks together. School felt pretty lonely without him, which was strange in a school with over two thousand pupils.

After his PE lesson, Mr Strachan came over and spoke to him.

'Have you started your Community Service yet?'

'No, not yet. I should start in a couple of weeks.'

'Where's Robbie? I haven't seen him for a couple of days.'

'He's moved to someplace in Wales, because of his dad's job.'

'Good. I always thought he was a bad influence on you. Perhaps now you can concentrate on your schoolwork and get some decent qualifications.'

'Maybe he'll get some qualifications, going to a school in Wales?'

'Robbie's chances are probably exactly the same, wherever he goes to school.'

'But in a small school, he'd get more one-to-one attention, wouldn't he?'

'No doubt. And some small schools have excellent track records. But even with undivided attention, he'd only amount to as much as he wanted to. He doesn't appear to have any inner drive or ambition.'

Luke didn't think that Mr Strachan's comments were justified but wasn't sure how to defend Robbie. As he wandered off to his next class, he wondered why he hadn't mentioned that he would be going to the same village in Wales, thanks to Damian mucking things up as usual.

Chapter 24 – In the Village – Cannabis Plants

As soon as it got dark enough Joey and James decided that they should sneak down to the field where Tommo had planted the cannabis and try and destroy it. They had filled several bottles with vinegar and washing-up liquid and packed them into a rucksack.

It was dark and cold, so Joey used the torch facility on his mobile phone to make sure they didn't fall into any ditches or potholes on the way. As they got closer to the cabin they could see a faint glow of light from the window, so they turned their torch off. They couldn't hear anything so they hoped Tommo would be too spaced-out to hear them. They were both nervous and making each other jittery. They left the bag at the edge of the field and grabbed a bottle each and walked quickly and quietly towards the crop. Crouching down, they took opposite ends and started spraying the plants. They kept stopping every couple of seconds, jumping at every sound around them.

'I think that will have to do for now. We might have to come back and finish off the rest of them when it's a bit lighter,' said James.

'That could be risky. What if Tommo catches us?' Asked Joey.

'We'll have to be really careful. Maybe we could wear better clothes and thick gloves next time. And we need to tackle the ones in the shed.'

Suddenly a light appeared nearby, and they realised that Tommo had opened the door of the shed. Worried that they had been caught they crouched down as low as they could, then waited as they realised Tommo was relieving himself nearby. James glared at Joey when he started fidgeting. They waited for ages till he had finished and disappeared back inside, before heading back up the hillside.

After a series of interviews and tests, letters had been sent out to successful applicants giving them a Contract of Employment and a starting date on the new building site.

Joey ran upstairs with Paul's letter.

'Dad, you've got a letter, and it says "Private and confidential", do you want me to open it?'

'No. If it's marked private and confidential, that's because it's private – and confidential.' He tore the letter open and quickly read it.

'Great news boys, I've got the job as Senior Electrician. That means I'll be working with Rhodri and Gavin if they've been successful. I start next month.'

'Are you going to tell William?'

'I think I'll pop over and speak to him. Put some breakfast on boys, I'll be back in a while.'

Shortly afterwards Paul returned.

'How did it go?'

'Badly. He couldn't remember our conversation about me working on the building site and accused me of deliberately getting him drunk.'

Chapter 25 – In the City – The War of the Roses

As they would be living in a small caravan at the building site for several months, Luke had been told he would only be able to take the really important things. He was taking a couple of overflowing bin bags down to the dustbins when he noticed that the mural had been changed again. This time it displayed a huge green field with a flag raised on it. The flag had blue and white vertical stripes. Underneath it was the words to a song:

We had joy, we had fun,
We had Tesco's on the run,
But the joy didn't last,
Cos Councillors' votes have now been cast.

The double doors that had previously been the turnstile were painted black, and written in huge red letters were the words, The War of the Roses. On the left-hand door, the red rose of Lancashire County Cricket Club had a skull and crossbones superimposed over it, and the right had what appeared to be a cheap bunch of white roses in a Tesco's carrier bag, held aloft by a caricature of Phil Clark, Tesco's Chief Executive. The residents near the Old Trafford County Cricket Club were upset because Tesco had somehow been granted planning permission to build a huge superstore on the only piece of grass in the area. There were petitions and meetings with the local Council, but it seemed as if Tesco would soon be trying to turn the area into a building site.

Chapter 26 – In the Village – The Sex Pistols

It was a warm, spring morning and the first day that Paul would start working on the building site. Joey woke up in great spirits, thundering down the stairs as though he were being chased by the devil.

'Morning dad, what's for breakfast? Have you made me my lunch? Can you help me with my art homework?' James followed him and reminded him that this was their first breakfast together in ages. 'Calm down and just eat your breakfast for once.'

'Morning Joey, slow down a bit. What makes you think I can help you with your art homework?' asked Paul.

'Well it's all about your era' replied Joey.

'You mean it's renaissance period then?' joked James.

'No, it's all about punks. I need to get some pictures for a collage, but I don't know the names of any of the groups to search for.'

'Well there's the Sex Pistols and The Clash; you should be able to get loads of good pictures from that period,' Paul enthused. 'I was a bit of a punk, but Granny went mad when I brought a Dead Kennedys record home. She was convinced that I was going to get my hair shaved into a Mohican and start having piercings done.'

'You, a punk? I don't believe it. You're far too sensible, and besides, you only ever listen to music by Springsteen and Seal. Hardly rebellious stuff is it?' said James.

'Hey, you should listen to Springsteen's 41 shots, and I had my moments. I once joined a protest march against the bombs at Greenham Common,' said Paul.

'Where?' Asked James and Joey together.

'They were trying to store nuclear bombs at Greenham Common, and the protests lasted for years during the 80s. That's where I met your mum; she was always trying to put the world to rights.'

'I miss Mum,' said Joey quietly.

James gave him a hug 'I know you do, buddy, we all do.'

Paul hugged Joey and clipped James affectionately around the ear. 'I'll see you tonight, and make sure to get your homework done this evening, not in the morning, ok?'

'Do you think they might have a part-time job for me once the houses are built? Maybe working in the sales office or something?' Asked James.

'I'm not sure. But the Sales office will be a cabin on the site. One of the first jobs I will be doing will be to connect the electricity supply for them. There's a guy called Andrew Sumner-Smith, he's the Build Manager. I'll ask him.'

'Great, thanks.'

Paul picked up his lunch and his hard hat and strolled down to the building site.

Joey quickly finished his homework and grabbing his school bag, started running for the bus to school. He saw one of William's sheep on the road, and after running after it for a couple of minutes he eventually cornered it. He grabbed it under its stomach and dropped it over the wall into the field. He decided he would have to warn William that he must have a hole in a fence somewhere and ran over to William's farm. Parked outside, in pristine condition, was Reg's Jaguar. Reg lived less than a mile away, so it seemed strange for him to have driven to William's farm. Joey's imagination went into overdrive, so he sneaked along the edge of the barn and saw Reg and William talking. He couldn't hear everything, just little snippets, but the general gist seemed to be:

'I've got a strong young man who would like to do some work around the village, and I thought you would appreciate the help,' said Reg.

'Well, I might be interested. Who is it; it's not Work Experience is it? They did more harm than good last time.'

'No, it's not Work Experience, but it's something similar. It's a young lad who has to do some community service.'

'What, a criminal working here? No thanks,' shouted William.

'He was a shoplifter. He just stole some cigarettes. He knows he did wrong, but he's repentant, and now he wants to pay for his crime. It's up to us to allow him to repay his debt to society. But if you don't need any help on the farm, that's fine. I'm sure there are plenty of other worthy causes in the village,' Reg said.

'Who is this person, and what kind of jobs will he be able to do?' asked William.

'His name is Luke Mills; his father is working on the new development. He could repair walls and fences, and I'm sure there are other jobs that you could give him. You would be doing him a favour, teaching him skills like drystone walling and larch fencing. It would be a terrible shame for your skills to die out.'

'I'm not sure.'

'Well, how about a short trial, say, a couple of hours for one or two days? If it doesn't work out, there's no harm done.'

'Alright, but will he be supervised by anyone else? I mean, suppose he's aggressive? I'm not as fit as I used to be.'

'He'll be introduced to you by a supervising officer, who will stay with you both for the first session. You can then mutually agree on a time for any further appointments, assuming you're happy to continue.'

'Fine, when will the first meeting be?'

'I'll get his supervisor to ring and arrange a time with you. The lad could probably also help tidy up your driveway for you.'

That was the last thing that William wanted to hear. He couldn't understand what the fuss was about his driveway; it was perfectly fine as far as he was concerned.

'There is nothing whatsoever wrong with my driveway.'

'I just meant fill in the potholes, so they don't damage your vehicles, and tidy up a bit. You don't want to let the village down do you?'

'In what way am I letting the village down, exactly? Things have been hard for a few years, and it's not getting any easier.'

'That's why it will be helpful for you to have this strapping young lad helping around the farm, I'll pop round in a few days and you can let me know how it's going, alright?'

Distracted by the news, Joey forgot to have a conversation with William about the sheep and walked back to the road and waited for the bus to school. He wondered if he should mention to Catherine that a shoplifter was going to be working for William. He hadn't met a shoplifter before, but in his imagination, he was on a par with Murray 'The Hump' Humphreys, a member of Al Capone's gang, supposedly the architect of the Valentine's Day Massacre. He originated in Wales, not far from Rowan and he still had relatives living in the area. With his imagination in full flow, Joey hopped on the bus, thinking of big-city gangsters hiding somewhere like Rowan.

Chapter 27 –The Move to the Village

'Come on, Luke, hurry up,' shouted his mum. 'We're lucky to be able to move to the village.'

'Yeah, dead lucky,' snarled Luke. He was trying to imagine how cramped things were going to be in the caravan. It only had one bedroom, and he would have to make up his bed every night on the seats in the living room. There was storage space beneath the settee, where he could keep his clothes. Their flat-screen, high-definition television was far too large for the caravan, so they would be using a crappy little thing that he would connect his Xbox up to. He would only be able to play on it between coming home from school and when Damian got home, as Damian liked to take sole custody of the remote control.

The shower was tiny and so was the toilet, which was unfortunately opposite the compact kitchen. The toilet could be emptied in one of two ways; either by parking over a specially designed drain; or by taking the cartridge out and emptying it. He had to try and remember not to do any 'number twos' if he could help it.

Damian was driving his old Ford Capri, which was gold and black, with rust highlights. He was useless at remembering he was towing a caravan and got irrationally angry with people who beeped their horns at him when he pulled out without taking into consideration the additional distance needed for the caravan.

Luke had sent a text to Robbie.

'Guess where I'm on my way to?' But he had not received a reply.

The nearer they got to Rowan, the worse his signal was. Therefore, Luke consoled himself with the idea that Robbie may not have received his message or been able to send a response.

When they got near to the village, they had to drive over two small, single-lane bridges, along a winding, country lane, over a cattle grid and into a field. The building site itself was fenced off with high silver-coloured fencing, and the ground was a huge grassy area with plots marked out with blue spray paint that looked familiar, and tape, rather like crime scenes.

There were already half a dozen caravans parked up, of varying ages and sizes. Some were pretty scruffy, apart from the first one which was white with an apple green stripe down the side, and an apple green awning. After some manoeuvring, Damian lined up the caravan parallel to the last one. It was a bit too close to the other one for Beth's peace of mind, but after the journey from hell, she didn't want to ask him to move it again.

Beth offered to start unpacking the crockery whilst Damian and Luke explored the area. However, Damian was keen to watch the football as there were only half a dozen games left until the end of the season and Manchester United could still potentially take the title. Luke, feeling brave, decided to go and have a wander about on his own.

However, seeing nothing but fields, hills and sheep for miles was a bit weird. He was worried about going out into the countryside and getting lost. There were a series of little lanes that ran off in different directions, but there didn't seem to be any signs anywhere or obvious landmarks like pubs, schools, launderettes or streets of houses.

He hadn't mentioned to any of his friends that he was moving because he wasn't sure how they would respond. He tended to hang around with them when Robbie was not available, which he thought probably made him a terrible friend.

He was wondering how else to make contact with Robbie. He had even tried to ring him a couple of times but hadn't been able to get hold of him. It felt strange because even when they hadn't spoken face to face in the past, they had always texted or communicated via their Xbox Live connection. Even Robbie's brother Scott hadn't been on the Xbox for days.

He wandered down to a stream and peered into it. He could see that further up steppingstones had been placed haphazardly across it. He crossed to the other side and watched some sheep in the field with their lambs. One or two of the lambs were bouncing about on all fours, as if they were spring-loaded, which made him smile. After a while, he started to get a bit cold so decided he should head back to the caravan.

His mum seemed quite cheerful. 'Well, what do you think of the area?' She asked.

'It's too quiet and depressing. How am I going to make friends when it doesn't seem as if there are any other kids around here?'

'There will be kids. You just haven't met them yet.'

'But what will we do, where will we go? There doesn't seem to be anywhere to just hang out.'

'There will be loads of places, and just think, you'll be able to do loads of cross-country running. Your PE teacher said you loved all that,' she said encouragingly.

'Do you mean they'll have clubs or something like that?' he asked.

'I've no idea; maybe you could start one if there isn't one already.'

Luke didn't think that was likely but decided to let the matter drop.

'Well, Damian is still glued to the television, so why don't we walk into the village to buy some bits and pieces from the corner shop?' Beth suggested.

Luke couldn't imagine anything worse than staying in the caravan with Damian so agreed with the minimum amount of enthusiasm. He strolled down the lane with his mum and soon saw the outline of some houses and a pub. He couldn't imagine the kinds of goings-on that were associated with The Old Crow being carried out here. It looked utterly boring. He opened the door to the shop. It was pretty cluttered and overcrowded with all sorts of stuff. The counter was at the back and appeared to run almost the length of the room and through into next door which was a small café. As his mum picked up a basket and started filling it Luke wandered around. There was no queue in the shop, but they had to wait to be served as the assistant was serving in the café. She thanked them for waiting and explained she was short-staffed and had to

143

keep running between the shop and the café to serve in both. Beth mentioned to Luke that it would be great if she could get a job there.

Chapter 28 – Dry Stone Walls

It was Saturday morning and Luke's community supervisor rang him to let him know that he had arranged an initial meeting with William Llewellyn. Mr Deacon would be going with him, and together they could agree on a timetable of work that would suit everyone. Luke was anxious, and his palms were sweating. He had no idea what Mr Llewellyn was like, and he had no experience of working on a farm. In fact, he had no experience of work of any kind. He just hoped he wouldn't have to milk cows or do anything with pigs; they seemed like huge smelly animals and he didn't think he could touch them without cringing. He dressed in his best jeans and trainers and gelled his hair. Mr Deacon picked him up at ten o'clock and he drove Luke over to William's farm.

William showed them around the farm, explaining that he had let a lot of the land go in the past five years, although he hadn't wanted to It still appeared vast to Luke, but he could understand William's disappointment. He knew how strange it felt going past The Old Trafford Cricket Ground and seeing hoardings going up so that the green pitches could be sacrificed to a Tesco supermarket.

He was relieved to find out that there were neither pigs nor cows. However, there was a large flock of sheep and he'd seen a film where they were doing sheep shearing. It seemed like a job for strong men, and he thought if he had to do that, he might build his muscles up a bit. He tried to imagine himself in a checked shirt holding a sheep between his legs and using a huge razor to remove its fleece but couldn't conjure up the image.

William explained that part of his land was bought by a guy called Fred and his family from the city who wanted to get back to nature. They didn't have much knowledge and hadn't done much research before they bought the land, and there had been quite a few incidents with them. William thought it was amusing that they were surprised at how noisy it was in the countryside. They complained about a nearby farm that had a cock crowing and cows walking along the lane early in the morning when they were going to be milked. The dairyman had offered to put slippers on them as a joke.

William explained about the problem that he'd been having with Fred's sheep escaping from his field because the wall needed repairing, and William was fed up with finding them around his trough eating food put out for his flock.

'How do you know his sheep from yours?' asked Luke.

'Well, I mark mine with a blue stripe across their backsides, and Fred marks his with a red cross on their neck,' explained William.

'I once found several of Fred's sheep on the road, and Fred had said, (trying to use an upper-class English accent) 'I don't know how they're managing to get out; I can't see a gap anywhere.' 'So I walked the perimeter with him and found several tufts of wool on the bottom of the fence. I had to explain that they could wriggle underneath and that the wool was an indication of where

146

they were escaping. Not many people would be outwitted by sheep, but Fred was an exception to the rule.' William sounded despairing.

The majority of William's sheep were kept in fields that had dry-stone walls rather than fences, as they were much stronger. He then spent half an hour explaining the technique for repairing the dry-stone wall, choosing the right size stones and wedging them together.

After showing them the land William had taken them into the farmhouse. He had taken the precaution of hiding anything of value, including a picture of his wife that was in a silver frame. William made a pot of tea. He handed large mugs around and a plate of scones that he had been saving for his son and daughter-in-law, who he expected later that day. He hoped they wouldn't eat them all, but Luke tucked in; he was starving. He reminded William of his son Kenny when he was younger. Of course, Kenny wouldn't dare eat so enthusiastically now; his wife would be appalled. She always insisted that they use the best china, which William preferred to keep for special occasions. He'd already broken a few pieces when he'd washed them in the past year or so, to his utter disappointment. Melissa was keen to use the plates but somewhat less keen to help with the washing up, possibly because her manicures cost more than some families spent on food for a week.

'So when can I start?' asked Luke.

'Well, I thought tomorrow for an hour or two,' replied William.

'Can't I start now? I could just repair the wall at the front of the driveway,' he said eagerly. Luke could sense William's suspicion and he was trying to create a good impression.

'Well I won't be able to help much; I'm expecting my son and his wife shortly,' said William.

Luke thought he seemed a bit miserable at the prospect. 'Well, as long as Mr Deacon has no objections, I'll just come and make sure you know exactly what to do.'

'It's alright, I think I can remember,' said Luke breezily as he went outside.

He worked steadily for an hour. His sections didn't look quite as uniform as the previous wall, but it was strong and secure. It was quite nice being out in the fresh air and he was hoping that William would be pleased with him.

Just as he was moving onto the next gap in the wall, a spotlessly clean Jaguar drove past him. There were two people in the car and they both stared at him as they passed. They were so intent on Luke that they apparently didn't notice the huge puddle they went through, which splashed him so that he was soaked from the waist down. Luke's good humour evaporated immediately. He wanted to run up the lane after them and say something, but he thought they might be William's family and decided to let it go. He finished the last piece of the wall and then went to speak to William to let him know that he would be back the next day. He didn't think he would want to do it for a living but couldn't believe how satisfying he had found the work.

As he approached the farmhouse, he could hear urgent, angry whispers. 'He could steal all your money. You can't trust a criminal like that; you don't know anything about him.'

This was from Kenny, and Melissa then piped up with, 'He could murder you and bury you in one of the fields when no one's around.'

William shouted back, 'I have hidden all my valuables, so you can stop worrying.' Luke was surprisingly hurt by William's remark.

Luke left the tools outside the farmhouse and, as he passed the Jaguar, he was tempted to do something to the car. However, he resisted the urge and walked home feeling miserable. In the distance, he saw a couple of dodgy-looking men who reminded him of the ABA, with a young lad in a red hoody. They were shouting and pushing him around. Reluctant to get involved, he put his head down and walked quickly on. He wasn't expecting this kind of conflict in the village.

His mum was horrified when she saw the state of his clothes.

'I thought you were only going for a chat. I didn't think he was going to make you start work straight away. I've got a good mind to go up there and have a word with him.'

'Mum it's alright. I asked if I could get started straight away; he didn't make me.'

'Well, what were you thinking? Your last good pair of jeans and trainers are covered in mud.'

'I'll wear some old clothes tomorrow, don't worry.'

'But you haven't got any old clothes; you'll have to take something of Damian's.' He didn't want to wear something of Damian's but couldn't think of an alternative.

He was still feeling pretty stung by William's remark as he went to bed that night. As he dwelled on the comments, he tried to put himself in William's shoes. How would he feel if he had only just met someone who had been found guilty of shoplifting, and hadn't had an opportunity to get to know them properly? But he also tried to justify his feeling of betrayal. He couldn't think of a single occasion in his life when he had stolen something for himself. He fell asleep feeling confused and isolated.

When he awoke, he was feeling slightly less aggrieved. He wanted to prove to William that he could be trusted. He dressed in an old shirt and jeans belonging to Damian, and an old pair of trainers. As his mum came through for breakfast she glanced at Luke and smiled.

'Are you off up to the farm then?' Asking the obvious.

'Yes, I'll probably work for a couple of hours. I should be back by lunch.'

'Well, alright then. Try to make a good impression, he might be able to give you paid work, like a Saturday job, after you've finished your Community Service.' He had a bowl of cereal and then walked up to the farm.

As he was on his way, he saw two boys slithering and running down the side of the hill. They shouted hello, and then ran along the road towards the village. Instead of ambling along, Luke then started running up to the farm. When he arrived, William came out to meet him, with an old sheepdog at his side. Luke was wary after the conversation he had overheard the day before and was unsure about the quality of his workmanship. He was relieved when William said, 'It's alright boyo, there's no need to rush. This wall's been here for over a hundred years, and judging the way you've patched it up, it should last another hundred and more.' Luke didn't think he could explain why he wanted to run so he didn't try.

'Have you had any breakfast?' William asked.

'Yes I've had Choco-loco loops,' said Luke.

'I don't know what that is, but it doesn't sound like it will keep you going for long. Come along into the kitchen and I'll give you a proper breakfast.' He followed William, and the smell of food cooking made his mouth water. Luke could see sausages and two slices of bacon grilling. He told William that his mother used to work in a sausage factory, where she added the rusks to the mixture.

'Well, butchers tend not to add much to sausages here in the country. It's the same with bacon; we don't add all that nitrate and nitrite stuff that they do in supermarkets,' informed William.

'Why do the supermarkets add that stuff if they don't need to?' asked Luke.

'Well, it's usually to preserve it longer, I think. They often have bacon sitting around in those plastic bags for weeks, whereas we don't tend to do that here. Another thing they add, which is completely inessential, is water to meat. They do that to make it weigh more, which is completely dishonest. But when you let the meat defrost, you can see it sitting in water. That wouldn't happen if the factories hadn't injected the water into the chicken in the first place.'

As Luke took the plate which held bacon, eggs, sausages, mushrooms and tomatoes he tried to remember a time when he had eaten vegetables at breakfast but couldn't. It looked and smelt great and he tucked in and ate everything in front of him.

When they had finished Luke followed William up to the stream where they were going to repair the willow fencing. He could see where the bank was eroded and how the willow provided a natural habitat for creatures and insects. He noticed that the stream ran along the back of William's vegetable plot, and he listened attentively as William explained why he cultivated plants so that certain insects would be attracted to them, which in turn would eat the greenfly that often damaged crops. He couldn't help wishing that lessons were this interesting.

'This way I don't need to use chemicals, so everything that I grow is organic,' explained William

Luke asked several questions which William was happy to answer.

'Do you know the two lads I've seen running around here?'

'Yes, they're James and Joey Jones who live further up the hill. Do you like running?'

'Yes, I liked cross-country running at school, but none of my mates did,' he admitted.

'Well, you should take part in the annual cross-country race, but you need to start training. It's held at the end of spring, so you've not got long to prepare.'

Luke was surprised as William then pointed to the hill where the event would start and explained the route and how long it could take to complete it. 'It's quite a scramble; it's not like running on one of your fancy treadmill things. And they don't run in smart trainers either; they all wear spikes.'

'Where would you buy those round here?'

'Oh, you would have to go into the main town, but they would be able to kit you out completely in proper clothes,' said William.

'What do you mean proper clothes?'

'Well jeans are pretty impractical, aren't they?' asked William.

'Impractical,' Luke gasped. 'I thought they were supposed to be practical.'

'Well, they're heavy, but not warm. For working, you need natural materials like cotton, which is lightweight, or something waterproof. If your jeans get wet, they'll be soaking and heavy for hours.' Luke bristled as he remembered his soaking from the day before. 'James will tell you where to get stuff from.'

Luke casually asked about the runners taking part in the race. 'James and Joey are both taking part this year. James is a favourite; he's eighteen. Joey is fifteen, but he's a champion little runner. I often see him running to school and training with his brother at the weekends. Their dad, Paul, won it a few years on the trot too. If you take part you'll need to keep your eye on Huw and Lloyd, they're not to be trusted.'

Looking back over the route Luke didn't think he would be able to enter such an event; it seemed pretty gruelling, and nothing like the Manchester or London marathons.

Luke heard the familiar beep of his mobile as he received a text. It was the first one he had received in days, so he assumed it was because he was higher up the hillside. It was from Robbie, 'I know where you are.' He tried to remember what he had last said to Robbie, so he scrolled back up and read it. He could hardly believe he still hadn't seen or spoken to Robbie even though they had both been in the village for a couple of days.

As Luke and William started to make their way down the hillside, they could just make out someone sitting on the wall. They watched as he idly picked up some stones and started to throw them near his feet. Then he started to throw with some force, at a group of sheep, until he hit one of them in the eye. The sheep bleated as though it were in terrible pain and ran away. They watched as several of the sheep ran away and started grazing on the far side of the hill.

'I'd better get Dylan and round up the sheep before he does any more damage.'

'Who's Dylan?'

'He's my sheepdog.'

'Okay, well I'll see you tomorrow.'

'Fine, see you tomorrow.'

As he got nearer, Luke recognised Robbie. He felt awkward at the thought of William seeing him with

Robbie, so he ran over to him as soon as William disappeared around the corner of the farmhouse.

'Hiya, are you surprised to see me?' Asked Luke.

'No, my mum bumped into your mum. She's going sick. She only wanted to move here to get away from you!' Robbie replied.

'Thanks.' Luke didn't mention that his mum had felt the same way about Robbie.

'Where have you been all day?' asked Robbie.

'I've been doing my community service. Do you see this wall? I fixed it, here and here. And the fence over there. Now the sheep from next door can't get in and nick the food from William's flock.'

'You sound weird, and you look weird; what are you wearing?'

'I didn't want to wreck my clothes, so I wore Damian's,' said Luke defensively.

'Alright, but I don't want to be seen in public with you dressed as a cowboy. Get changed then come round to mine. It's the biggest caravan on the plot, obviously! I've got that new street-fighting game.'

'I thought you didn't have enough money for it.'

'I didn't, but Scott did. He's contributed to it but he doesn't know yet. I've raided his piggy bank.'

'What if he was saving up for something?'

'It's tough!'

Chapter 29 – New School

Luke had been shown where to get the bus to school, and he was up and dressed quite early for a change. It was probably partly because he could hear all kinds of animals, from a cock crowing; to birds in nearby gardens; to sheep making all kinds of odd noises.   There was less disturbance in a pub in the middle of Ardwick at throwing-out time.

Robbie pulled a sausage roll from his pocket, and Scott joined him a few minutes later. Luke would have called for them, but he knew Sandra would inevitably be at the caravan, polishing and washing.

'What do you think the school's going to be like?' asked Luke.

'Don't know. Don't care,' replied Robbie. 'All I know is that we are going to have to make an impression on the new kids. Let them know who's boss.'

'Err, we're the new kids.'

As they were waiting for the bus, they were joined by Joey. He stood awkwardly to one side and then eventually introduced himself to them. Scott was pleased to meet him and was open and friendly. Robbie just shrugged and said "hiya" and then carried on eating his sausage roll. When he'd finished it he threw the paper bag onto the roadside. Joey was shocked, it added to his feeling of wariness towards the incomers.

On the journey to school, Luke half-listened to Robbie as he let him know how he planned to conduct himself at the new school. Luke couldn't fathom out why Robbie wanted to make enemies of everyone.

Joey sat next to Scott and they talked the whole way. Scott told him about his interest in cosmology and the planets. How he hoped the clear skies would help as there would be less light pollution. Joey was pretty shocked when Scott went on to tell him about the threat he had faced from the ABA, including how he had personally been attacked when he was suspected of painting over the graffiti.

'We don't tend to get graffiti around here,' said Joey.

'I quite like it, when it's done well. And it is the only thing that Spud did well, to be honest,' said Scott. 'He's a thug and he tries to push kids to sell drugs for him. That's probably something else you don't have here.'

'Actually, we've had a problem with Tommo who tries to sell drugs, he uses social media.'

Scott looked surprised but didn't have time to discuss the subject in detail as they were approaching the school.

When they jumped off the bus, Luke, Robbie and Scott couldn't believe how small it was. The lavatories were in a separate brick building to the side of the main classrooms, and there were only three toilets in each, plus three small wash-hand basins. They could see the fields and hills behind the school. However, the playground at the front of the school was a small concrete area, which was overlooked by the staffroom. Luke wondered where Robbie would be able to have a secret smoke; there wasn't much room in the toilets. At his old school, there were usually about fifty kids smoking in various areas around the school, during break times. He was pretty certain that Robbie wouldn't last all day without a fag.

Chapter 30 – First Lesson

Joey pointed Scott in the direction of his classroom and showed him where they would all eat lunch. 'Do we stay in the same room for every lesson?' Scott wanted to know.

'Yes of course, why not?' Asked Joey.

Scott explained that previously he had to attend his form room for registration; another for assembly; and separate rooms for every single subject, which were often in different blocks. Joey pointed out that most of his subjects would be taught by one teacher until he started doing his GCSEs.

'Okay. Well, why aren't you carrying anything? I'm used to carrying a bag full of books, my PE kit, pencil case, lunch, keys, mobile and wallet every day.'

'We leave a lot of stuff here at school. I leave my trainers here for months and I only take my PE kit home when I remember to.'

'Well, what about your wallet and your mobile?'

'I don't bring any money because there's nothing to spend it on. The bus is free, and I bring a packed lunch. I've got an old mobile, but I usually leave it at home, I only use it in emergencies. I'd love a smartphone, my dad said I can't have one until I'm 16.'

Joey was impressed as Scott demonstrated the way he had set up his favourite playlist, showed off his Spotify account; and how he could listen to audiobooks at various speeds. He raised his eyebrows slightly when Scott mentioned that Robbie often used that functionality when he had to read a book for English.

He then led Luke and Robbie to their classroom, which held just twenty desks.

Luke snorted in disgust when he realised there was only a single computer in the room, which was on the teacher's desk. He couldn't imagine how IT lessons would be conducted. His previous school had a computer on every desk with the latest software installed, as well as several top-of-the-range colour printers in every IT suite, of which there were at least four or five. He compared his old science lab which contained all of the latest equipment to this dump where all of the equipment fitted into four large cupboards along one wall. The teacher, Mr Edison, entered the room and introduced himself to Luke and Robbie. He then asked them to sit at two of the desks at the front of the room, next to a desk that had no chair in front of it. A young lad called Sam wheeled up to the desk and introduced himself to them both.

They were old-fashioned desks made of wood that had several decades of pupils' names engraved on them. One or two enterprising souls had tried to use bubble writing – if only Spud could see this now, thought Luke.

By mid-morning, Luke realised Robbie was holding his mobile underneath the desk, texting Scott that he was bored and feeling the need for a cig. Luke glanced at him as Mr Edison asked him a question that he didn't understand, and he was shouted at to sit up and pay attention. Looking through the window at the physical features in the landscape as Mr Edison explained the different terms. He pointed out examples of scree and the devil's kitchen. Further afield Luke could see some of the mountains of Snowdonia; some were rocky and some appeared to be covered in a forest of different coloured trees. The top peaks were scattered with snow. He could even just make out a waterfall. It was the first time Luke could recall enjoying a geography lesson; although Luke had no intention of showing too much enthusiasm in front of Robbie.

He was secretly pleased when Mr Edison told them that the following week they would be having a field trip and would see a burial chamber and an Iron Age hill fort with drystone ramparts. Robbie asked how much it would cost and was surprised when he was told it would be free. To make sure that he understood, he asked if the school had its own minibus, as he hadn't seen one. His disappointment was audible when he discovered that they would be walking all the way there and back.

'What? Surely you don't expect us to walk all that way!' he exclaimed.

'Why not? It's only a couple of miles, and most of it would be inaccessible by a vehicle anyway,' replied Mr Edison.

'Well, we're not going all that way by foot! And what about Sam, if he's sitting it out, I'll stay with him,' he replied.

Mr Edison, concerned that there might be a rebellion on his hands, addressed the whole class. 'Have any of you got serious objections to walking as far as Capel Garmon? And what about you Sam?' he asked. There were some smirks aimed at Robbie and they all responded that it would be a great relief from the classroom.

'I'll use my chair as far as I can, then my sticks. If it's too rocky I'm happy to be carried.'

The tallest lad in the class, Kieran added, 'I'll just throw him over my shoulder!'

Robbie persisted, 'Well me and Luke are not going. We could fall down the side of the mountain and die, and we would sue this school for every penny it's got.'

Luke seemed uncertain, and Mr Edison pounced on the opportunity to increase the division between the two new boys, so he addressed Luke. 'You appear to be a fit young lad; would you have a problem walking as far as Capel Garmon? It's not as though you would be climbing to the top of Snowdonia; we will only be going as far as the burial chamber, then walking along to the fort.'

Before Luke could respond Robbie interrupted with 'You say that now, but when we're out there, you'll start saying, oh we'll just head up the mountain a little bit.'

'That would be ridiculously ambitious boyo, I wouldn't dream of taking you up a mountain. You're neither fit nor strong enough,' he replied.

Robbie splurted, 'I'm a lot stronger than you and these skinny wimps.' The skinny wimps raised their eyebrows and someone mumbled, 'I'd like to see him doing chin-ups against Sam!' Causing more sniggers.

Luke was relieved when Mr Edison ended the matter by saying that if Robbie felt up to it, he would be allowed to prove that he was stronger than everyone else. If the smirks of the other pupils had been audible, he would have been deafened.

When they got out into the tiny playground, Robbie rounded on Luke. 'I can't believe you really want to go climbing up a mountain. And why didn't you stick up for me?'

'It's not climbing up a mountain; you heard him. We'll just be down in the valleys, so stop panicking,' Luke tried to mollify him.

'But you still could have stuck up for me and told him that you didn't want to go,' argued Robbie.

'But I do want to go. We get out of class for a few hours, we don't have to do any work, we don't have to answer any questions, or do any writing,' said Luke.

'Well, I don't do any of that anyway. I'd rather just sit at the back of the class and listen to Spotify,' rumbled Robbie.

'Somehow I don't think we're going to get away with that here,' said Luke.

'Just keep your eyes open, I'm going to the toilet for a cig,' and Robbie stormed off.

Chapter 31 – The Shoplifter

Joey had to nip into Catherine's shop for some ingredients for a cake he was making at school the next day. The school policy was that they would provide unusual ingredients and pupils would buy their own. This saved having problems dealing with individual needs and allergies. He gathered all the items together, plus another bottle of vinegar, and holding them on his chest and tucked under his chin, he dropped them onto the counter.

'Morning Joey, how are you?'

'I'm fine thanks. How are you and your mum?'

'I'm fine. Mum's still a bit poorly, but one of the ladies who has moved into the caravans on the building site is coming to work for me, so mum can rest.'

'Oh, that's good news. Hope she can bake like you can.'

'Actually, I don't think she can, she didn't seem confident. So, I'm going to start her in the shop and I'll concentrate on the café.'

'Can't you teach her to cook?'

'I don't think I've got the time, and I'm not sure she's got the inclination. I think her family just prefers burgers and the like.'

'It's not that boy Luke's mum, is it?'

'I think so yes, why?'

'Well, I don't want to be mean, but he's a shoplifter. How do you know you can trust his mum?'

'Oh, Joey that's a terrible thing to say!'

'I know. I'm sorry. I probably shouldn't have said anything.'

'What makes you think he's a shoplifter?'

'He's doing Community Service up at William's farm for shoplifting. But I'm sure he wouldn't steal from you. He does seem nice enough.' He added hurriedly.

'Well, she's only on a week's trial. I'll see how we get on. But she seemed pleasant, and I like to think I'm a pretty good judge of character.'

'I hope it works out. And sorry for blurting that out.'

'That's alright, not to worry, I won't say anything. Let me know how the Victoria sandwich cake turns out.'

'I will. It's got to be better than James'. Do you remember his sank in the middle and got burnt around the edges?'

'I remember. I had to eat a piece and tell him it was delicious.'

'Well, I'll bring you a piece of mine.'

'Thanks.'

'Oh, and if you want to see a nice sight, Fred's out running. He should be coming past here soon, and he's wearing white shiny shorts.'

'And why would I want to see Fred running?'

'Dad said he's got a soft spot for you, and he's doing it for you.'

'Doing what for me?'

'The cross country race.'

'Oh, no. What do you mean he's wearing white shiny shorts?'

'I think they might be boxing ones.'

'What? You mean boxer shorts?'

'No, they're shiny like boxers wear.' Then he added as an afterthought as the door closed behind him 'or women.'

Chapter 32 – Luke and James meet

The next day, Luke got home from school, changed out of his uniform, and ran over to William's before Robbie had a chance to call for him. He was hungry but passed an apple tree on the way and, although it didn't appear to be in anyone's garden, he thought it might still be regarded as stealing. He didn't want to be thought of as a thief, and he didn't want to get in any more trouble whilst he was serving his community service order. Checking all around to make sure no one could see him, he helped himself to one of the least damaged apples on the floor.

When he got to William's, he found him standing in his garden with Joey. 'How did you get here so quickly?' asked Luke.

'Well, I didn't bother catching the bus; I ran home instead,' said Joey. 'I've been training for the local race, but I've just found out that you have to be sixteen to run that distance now. It's not fair; I'm easily as fit as most of the people around here,' he complained.

'I know, I've seen you running,' said Luke. 'Are you and your brother in a running club, do you have a trainer, and do you have to follow a programme?' he asked.

Joey, puzzled by all the questions, replied, 'Mostly we just run for fun. But we usually follow the route of the race as it's a bit difficult in parts, and it helps the more familiar you are with the terrain. It can be tricky with some of the uphill and downhill parts. Are you a good runner?'

'Well, I'm alright. I enjoyed the cross-country runs at my old school, but I can't imagine Mr Edison taking us cross-country running, can you?'

'Actually, he does. He will be entering the race, and he set the record years ago, which no one has broken yet.'

'You've got to be joking; he's ancient!' exclaimed Luke, realising too late that William was listening to their exchange. 'Sorry William, I didn't mean that in a bad way,' he stammered.

William couldn't think of a good way to interpret the remark or a suitable reply, so asked if they'd had any dinner. He sometimes fed Joey when his dad and James were going to be home late. He explained that he was going to make toad-in-the-hole, which he knew was Joey's favourite. Luke didn't know what it was, but it sounded appalling; however, he didn't want to show his ignorance. He was pretty certain that it wouldn't involve actual toads but thought it would have to be something green and disgusting like sprouts. 'I've also got loads of apples, so I thought I'd rustle up a nice apple crumble for pudding,' he added.

Luke decided that as Joey seemed pretty enthusiastic, it couldn't be too bad, and thought he could always hide something in his pocket if he couldn't finish it; he was wearing Damian's jeans, after all.

He still had the apple core in his hand and, wanting to appear thoughtful, asked William if he had a bin for it. William said that he could just throw it in the hedgerow. Remembering Joey's expression when Robbie dropped the paper bag, he hesitated. 'Won't that be littering?' he asked.

'Not really,' replied William. 'Dropping an apple core on an uncultivated piece of land like that, on balance you will be doing more good than harm. It's perfectly biodegradable; it will break down and just add compost to the other plants. If you put it in a bin, it will just be added to the landfill, which will take years to break down,' explained William.

'Oh, it's like the circle of life then. You know that scene in the Lion King when the young cub watches his dad get trampled to death by a stampeding herd of wildebeest,' suggested Luke.

'I have never seen it, but it sounds depressing,' said William. Joey grinned knowingly at Luke.

Luke watched William mix batter while some sausages were grilled. The smell was amazing. He rarely had sausages at home as his mum was sick of them by the time she came home from work. He was surprised by the sputtering as William added the mixture to a hot tin, which he took out of the oven, and then placed the sausages in a row in the batter.

Luke thought the half-hour that he had to wait for it to cook was the longest he had waited for a meal. Even Dylan was hanging around with his tongue out.

'While you tuck into that I'll make use of some of the apples. They'll go to waste if I don't use them soon.' Said William.

'Well why don't you just make loads of pies and freeze them all?' asked Luke.

'I haven't got a freezer, see, and I usually give Catherine half a dozen to sell in her shop, and she gives me the odd bottle of whisky. Fair exchange is no robbery, as they say.'

'Well, what if you fancy an apple pie in six months?'

'There are other apple trees around the village, and they all give their crops at different times of the year, so someone will be selling their pies to Catherine. But there aren't any that ripen during winter, so it makes you appreciate the first crop of the year. Oh and by the way, I wouldn't let Reg catch you taking his apples. Nobody else would mind, but Reg is a bit of a mean old sod.'

'How did you know it was one of Reg's apples?' he asked

'Well, it's a Cox's Orange Pippin, and there's only my tree and his in the village of that variety,' William explained.

'Well how did you know it was a Little Cock thingy?' asked Luke.

'Probably the same way you know different types of cars, I should think,' said William.

'I must admit there are a few nice 4x4s around here,' enthused Luke.

'Well you need vehicles like that around here, especially during the floods or when some of the main roads are blocked,' William replied.

'I noticed that nice Vectra next door; it's fit,' said Luke.

'Yes, that belongs to Fred. You can tell newcomers by how ridiculously inappropriate their cars are. I had to pull him out of a ditch with my tractor and tow him to the main road every day for a week during the snowy weather a couple of months ago. But I agree it's a pretty car, but pretty cars are not practical, working vehicles, are they?' asked William.

'Suppose not, but it's well banging,' agreed Luke. Although it didn't sound it, William assumed that was a positive term.

When they had all finished eating, William asked the boys if they would help him pick some more of the apples before they fell to the ground and got damaged. Joey grabbed the big basket and went outside, with William and Luke following him. Joey reached one of the lower branches and pulled himself up, scrambling easily up the tree. Luke tried to follow him. He attempted to pull himself up but merely kept swinging about and couldn't seem to find the strength in his arms to lift his body up. William and Joey exchanged a glance and to put him out of his misery William said that it would probably be best if he just grabbed the apples from the lowest branches as he was pretty tall. When they had finished, Joey jumped down from the tree and picked up the basket, which was nearly full. Luke thought that as he was the oldest of the boys, he should carry the basket, so he offered to take it. Joey passed it to him saying, 'If you don't mind.' Luke was amazed at the weight of all the apples and could barely carry them. As he struggled along behind them, he wondered at the strength and fitness of a skinny young boy like Joey. As he held the gate open for him, Joey realised that Luke wasn't as strong as he appeared and, without saying a word, took the basket back. Joey thought that as

Catherine was giving the newcomers the benefit of the doubt, he should too.

As they left William's and said goodbye, they saw James coming along the path. He introduced them to each other. Joey explained that Luke enjoyed running, and James asked if he would like to go out running with them sometime. 'Yeah great, when are you going?'

'After dinner if you like,' said James.

'We've already eaten with William,' explained Joey.

'It's alright for some. I don't suppose you've made anything for me and dad?' queried James.

'No, I didn't have time, but I did make a Victoria sandwich cake at school. It wasn't quite as badly burnt as yours.' He replied cheekily.

'Is it still in one piece?'

Joey then remembered he had run home from school but hadn't checked the condition of the cake. He had just dropped his bag in William's hallway. He hoped he would be able to salvage one nice slice for Catherine. He decided to change the subject.

'Luke and I have been helping William in his orchard, haven't we?' he asked Luke for confirmation.

'Yes, we picked a basket of apples,' explained Luke.

'One basket of apples took you two hours?' asked James incredulously.

'It was a big basket,' Luke tried to explain. The only brothers he had seen interacting close up were Robbie and Scott, and he had seen Robbie get angry with Scott for much less.

'I've seen the size of William's baskets,' said James jokingly. 'Anyway, I can meet you over by the footbridge and we can do part of the course if you like. In an hour or so?'

Relieved, Luke said, 'Fine, see you later.'

As they walked away up the hillside, Luke could hear Joey saying, 'Well if you're cooking for you and Dad, I could probably manage a bit. You know how mean William can be with his portions, don't you?'

He could hear James laughing as he walked home, thinking that he would need to let the huge meal settle before he went running.

Chapter 33 – Plan B

James and Joey told their dad that they were going out for a run. They had placed their rucksack underneath a couple of coats in the hallway which they had filled with another two bottles of vinegar and washing-up liquid. They followed part of the route and then took off towards the shepherd's hut. When they got within sight of it they could see Tommo and someone else grabbing the plants from outside and taking them into the hut. Even from this distance, they could see that the plants looked reasonably green and healthy, so they hadn't suffered any lasting damage.

'I'm scared. I haven't seen that guy with the scars before,' James admitted.

'I haven't, he doesn't look as if he's from round here. A few of the kids at school have said they had seen 'gangsters' hanging around,' said Joey.

'I wonder what they want. Do you think he's using Tommo to run a county lines operation?' Asked James.

'I don't know, what is that?' Joey wanted to know.

'It's where drug dealers and gangs use kids to infiltrate smaller towns and villages to sell their drugs. We are only down the road from Manchester and Liverpool,' James explained.

'Wow. Might explain why Tommo is spending so much time at the hut.'

'That and the fact his mum is a lush.'

'True.'

'It doesn't look as if our plan worked, what should we do now?'

'We'll have to come up with a Plan B. We'll have to be extra careful if some kind of gang is involved.'

Chapter 34 – PE Lesson

As he was eating his breakfast Luke heard his 'phone beep to let him know that he had received a text. It was from Robbie letting him know that he was throwing a sickie and that Luke should too. He thought about it for a split second but he knew they would be doing a cross-country run today and was going to show the others that he wasn't useless at everything.

Luke ignored the text and went to school as usual. If Robbie asked afterwards, he would say that his mobile had died, so he didn't get the message until it was too late, or that he hadn't got reception on his 'phone. Scott wasn't at the bus stop, so he assumed Robbie had managed to convince him to stay off school as well. He met Joey at the bus stop, and they soon found they had quite a lot of common interests. Joey seemed to have revised his initial wariness towards Luke.

On the days they had PE, Mr Edison always did it as the first lesson, as he believed it woke everyone up and prepared them for the day ahead. The boys' changing rooms were small and cold, and Luke assumed the girls' must be the same. They consisted of plain white tiled walls and wooden benches around three sides of the room. The floor of the showers was covered in white tiles and the air was positively bleak. There was a small window high up that let in a constant stream of cold air. There were eleven boys in the class, (twelve when Robbie turned up) and they piled into the changing room. They all quickly got into their running gear. Sam had a close-fitting lycra top which caused his biceps to bulge. Instead of his regular wheelchair, he would be using his racing chair on the road so that he didn't have to slow down to move off pavements at junctions.

Luke couldn't believe it when he saw Mr Edison. He looked completely different out of his school-teacher clothes of brown trousers and knitted sweaters. Once he was in his running shorts and vest he was lean and toned. Luke followed Mr Edison and the rest of the boys across the playground. The girls in the class joined them and they ran out of the school grounds and along the main road through Llugwy. It was a cool, bright day and made Luke remember his nan's remark about enjoying running in the morning, though she obviously meant much earlier than this. There was hardly any traffic and he could see the shops were all built with the local slate and had colourful signs hanging outside with their names in Welsh and English.

As they passed through the town centre the road opened up to a housing estate. The road rose slightly, and they passed a beautiful open park. Shortly after that, they were running downhill and then quickly uphill again. On the edge of the town was The Towers, a lovely gothic mansion, which was now a hotel. Mr Edison pointed it out to Luke and mentioned that it boasted its own cinema and a Balinese bedroom. Apparently from the tower, you could see Puffin Island. Luke couldn't understand how Mr Edison managed to hold a conversation; he needed every ounce of oxygen to just keep breathing. He was only just keeping up with everyone and was surprised that he could run for miles on flat roads, but the introduction of a few small hills had him desperately trying to suck air into his lungs. Sam was pretty good at keeping pace with everyone but slowed down when they went uphill. Downhill was a different story, as long as there was no traffic, he flew passed everyone, he was pretty impressive.

As the group made the final run back to the school he saw a shallow river, with the sunlight glinting off it. He was reminded of Farah, who had run much further than this since he was a child. He sprinted back to the playground, overtook several of the others and was only just beaten by two of the older boys.

He stripped off and dashed into the shower, happy to have the cool water on his hot, sweaty face. For the first time, the shower didn't involve shouted insults, anyone being thrown in fully clothed, or slaps with a wet towel. The boys just got dressed and returned to the classroom. Luke asked himself, 'did these kids not know how to have fun?'

Chapter 35 – Beth's New Job

As the journey to school took about forty minutes, Luke had to wake up early to get a quick shower before Damian and his mum. It was his mum's first day working in the corner shop for Catherine, so everyone was rushing around, trying to get ready on time, and not bump into one another.

'It's a job in a crappy shop, for minimum wage! Why are you getting so stressed?' snapped Damian.

'Well, thanks for the support!' She snapped back and stormed out.

As Luke was making their packed lunches, Damian snarled at him. 'You don't need that much meat on the sandwiches, take it easy.'

'What's your problem? Did you get out of the wrong side of the bed?'

'No, you cocky little sod. Just hurry up and get out of my way.'

Luke grabbed his school bag and left before the atmosphere diminished to an even lower temperature. He couldn't help but wonder if something had happened to Damian on the building site. He hoped to God he would be able to keep this job. In the few years he had been part of their lives he had already held several jobs.

He could see the beginnings of several houses on the building site. The footings had been dug into the ground and the outer walls were being built.

Robbie and Scott had managed to make full recoveries from their mysterious one-day illness and were at the bus stop, as was Joey. As the bus drove along the narrow lane they saw Fred running. His face was bright red and he could barely lift his feet. His t-shirt was slightly too short and his belly peeped out beneath it. Unfortunately, he had on the same ridiculous white shorts that he had worn the previous day. They all watched him with surprised expressions on their faces.

'Who's that?' Asked Robbie.

'It's Fred. He owns the farm next door to William. He's a bit of an idiot. He knows nothing about farming, but acts like an expert,' said Joey.

'What's he running for?'

'He's practising for the cross-country run.'

'No kidding, why?'

'He wants to impress Catherine.'

'The fit bird in the café?'

'Err, yes.' Joey had always regarded Catherine as a sort of substitute mother and was not used to hearing her described in that way.

'My mum's just started working for her. She's just going to be helping out in the shop because she's not much of a cook,' added Luke.

'She's not bad,' replied Robbie.

Luke was quite pleased with the faint praise until Robbie added, 'As long as it's come out of a packet.'

'Well, I'm sure Catherine appreciates the help. Her mum's been ill for ages so she has to do most of the work on her own,' said Joey.

'Actually, my mum would like a job in the café, and she's a pretty good cook,' mentioned Scott.

Luke thought that would be a terrible idea, as he knew that Beth and Sandra didn't get along and working in such close proximity was bound to cause friction. They each blamed the other's son for getting their son into trouble with the police, and the last time they had attended court with the boys for a previous shoplifting offence, Luke could clearly remember the harsh words that had been spoken. Beth had worn a smart white blouse and a navy skirt, which was rather short and schoolgirlish. Sandra had said something to the effect that Beth should dress her age. However, as Beth had given birth to Luke when she was only fifteen, she was only thirty-one. She resented the fact that Sandra assumed that they were the same age.

'I've got some magazines if you want to borrow them. Then you can see what's in fashion Beth.'

'No thanks. If your clothes are anything to go by, they'll be catalogues for boy's clothes.'

At that point, a court official came to speak to them, but they both knew that it was only the end of the first round. They listened to his instructions and then moved back to the middle of the room.

Seconds out, round two.

Sandra opened with, 'These are not boys' clothes; these are designer casual wear.'

Beth countered with, 'I'm sure our Luke's got those trainers; perhaps they're bisexual or something.'

'I think you mean unisex,' replied Sandra, glancing down at her feet uncertainly.

181

They both fixed smiles on their faces as a young man entered the room, sat down and nervously picked at a fingernail.

Seconds out, round three.

'I'm not trying to be nasty, Beth, but I do think you could wear something a bit more fashionable.'

'My clothes may not be the latest fashion, but that is because I go for stylish, classic pieces, and besides, what gives you the right to pass judgement on anyone else's appearance?'

'Because I always make an effort to keep up with the latest trends.'

'That hardly qualifies you as an authority on the matter, particularly since you seem to be taking your fashion cues from random B-list celebrities.'

Sandra gasped, 'And what's wrong with that?' but unfortunately the case was called at that point so they had been forced to call a truce.

For once they all had a fairly uneventful day at school and a day off from William's farm, and Luke was looking forward to getting home to play on his Xbox, something he hadn't done for ages. He was hoping that he would be able to speak to all his old friends via the live connection. However, he had struggled to maintain a connection for any length of time. It was frustrating. He was almost tempted to call for Robbie but didn't want to face Sandra.

When his mum came home she brought some of the homemade soup that Catherine had made that day. It was minestrone. Damian and Luke had never tried it before.

Luke thought it was alright, but as usual, Damian thought it was disgusting.

Luke was half-listening as his mum told them about her first day in the shop. She mentioned that Sandra had popped in as she was putting white wine in the fridge. Sandra had ridiculed her for putting red wine next to it when everyone knew that red wine was served at room temperature. Beth had tried to bite her tongue but had eventually responded with, 'well we can't all be as cosmopolitan as you, but have you ever considered that you might have too close a relationship with the wine bottle?'

Then she told them about this woman who just went straight behind the counter and helped herself to a bottle of vodka. As Beth challenged her she waved her away and said, 'it's alright, I'm family, Catherine's sister Genevieve.' He couldn't help wondering if Genevieve resembled Catherine.

Chapter 36 – The Run

James and Luke had made arrangements to meet at the footbridge two or three times a week at six in the evening so they could train together. The entire course was fourteen miles, and pretty gruelling.

On the first evening, Luke had worn his trainers, which James had instantly decided were unsuitable. He had run home and got Joey's running shoes. They were scruffy and curled up at the toes.

The first part of the course started in the village where it was pretty flat. It went alongside the new houses which were beginning to take shape. Pretty soon it went around the side of a huge hill; some areas were quite gravelly whilst others were still grassy and a bit slippery. Although from a distance it seemed as though the path was straight, when they were on it they had to run uphill and then downhill quite sharply part of the way. It was much trickier than he expected, and Luke was surprised at how tired he was. He was relieved when James suggested they pause for a minute.

When they did the following section it was downhill nearly all the way, and Luke's shins were aching with the strain of the run. Then they had to run along a stream for quite a while, and part of it involved dodging huge outcrops of rocks sometimes in the middle of the route. Their feet and legs were soaking wet and even though it was a mild spring evening, they felt pretty cold and cramped.

The next part involved running through several acres of fields, then climbing over a stile and through a gate that only opened a small amount, which slowed them down completely. James explained that it was so that ramblers could walk through the field that contained livestock without the risk of them leaving the gate open.

They then moved on to the fifth section which was uphill all the way, and in some parts the route was so steep that they were nearly scrambling on their hands and knees. Before they rounded a sharp bend, James warned Luke that there was a low-hanging tree that had felled many an unsuspecting runner. He always dodged underneath it, but Joey liked to grab the lowest branch and swing under it Tarzan style.

After a short rest, they tackled the sixth section which was the one that they were convinced Huw Morgan had cheated on. It went from midway around one hill down to ground level, across a footbridge, and up the final hill. There was a route that you could take that would avoid the bridge, but as there was a steward at that point, it should be impossible to get a marker for completing the section. The final section was from the last hill down to the edge of town where the finish line was. Despite the different types of obstacles Luke found running around the village a completely different experience from running in Manchester.

After the run, Luke asked where he could get a pair of running shoes, and James told him that he would have to catch the bus at the weekend to one of the towns near the coast where they stocked all kinds of sporting and outdoor equipment. It was only about twenty miles away, but the buses only came once a day, so he would have to be ready at nine in the morning. The bus back only returned at three in the afternoon, so he would have to amuse himself for the whole day.

Luke decided to ask Robbie if he would like to come with him, as it had been a while since they had seen each other outside school. Luke felt a bit guilty as he had been spending time at the farm, even if it was to carry out his Community Service and running with James and Joey. He wasn't sure if Robbie was enjoying life in the village as much.

Chapter 37 – The Running Shoes

Luke had made an effort to get all of his homework done and any jobs around the caravan that his mum asked him to do. He was trying to stay in her good books so that he could ask her for some money for the running shoes. He got up early and picked up all of his clothes from the floor and put them into the laundry basket. His mum would take it to the launderette later that day. He made a pot of coffee, even though he didn't like the stuff, because he thought it might put his mum in a good mood to wake up to the smell of it freshly brewing.

He saw that there were some clothes that his mum had hand-washed, still in the sink, so he decided to hang them on the line. His mum managed to make it seem easy, and he was surprised at how awkward it was. He pegged one cuff of a shirt on the line, then the bottom of the shirt, but the other cuff was still trailing on the floor. He tried to fold one of his mum's skirts over the line, but it seemed to be still dragging in the grass so he placed it sideways on the line.

When he picked up Damian's jeans and tried to get a peg over the waistband, it wouldn't go, so he tried the bottom of one of the legs. The waistband was still dangling on the floor, so he put the other leg halfway over the line and stuck a peg in it. As he tackled another school shirt, he pegged one cuff and then the collar, but he had run out of line so he pegged the other sleeve back on top of the other cuff. He couldn't work out how his mum kept everything up off the grass and had failed to notice the big prop that she used to lift the line-up when she had finished.

As he came back into the caravan his mum wandered through to the kitchen. 'How come you're up so early? The last time you were up before me was when you wanted to watch something geeky on television.' Luke couldn't remember watching anything geeky on television but thought it might have been the London marathon. However, he didn't want to get into that right now so he just said that he hadn't been able to sleep and thought he would get up and finish his homework – a small lie.

'Well, I'm glad you did. Thanks for making the coffee; pour us both a cup will you love?' Luke didn't want one but thought his mum might think it was wasteful to make a huge pot just for her. He tried drinking it, but it was strong and bitter. He added another couple of teaspoons full of sugar, but it didn't improve the flavour much. Even his mum seemed to shudder when she drank it but didn't want to appear ungrateful. She even forced herself to drink two cups.

Luke decided to take the bull by the horns, so he said, 'Mum, you know I've been running with James? Well, I'm thinking of entering the annual cross-country race, do you mind?'

'Why would I mind love?' she asked.

'Well, I need a proper pair of running shoes, or I won't be able to enter.'

'What's wrong with your trainers? They're brand new.'

'They're fine for knocking about in, but because the route is a bit rocky and slippery I need something with a bit more grip.'

'Well, it's lucky that Catherine wants extra help in the shop. Should I put a good word in for you?'

'Hmm, well, ok. But only for a few hours at the weekend. I still want to be able to go training every night and I have to finish my Community Service.'

'Fine, but if you get your foot in the door now, she might be able to give you a full-time job when you finish school.'

Luke didn't think he'd like that at all but didn't think this was the time to mention it. He asked for some money for the running shoes. His mum could only spare fifty pounds, so he hoped that would be enough. He went to meet Robbie to catch the bus to town.

As the bus passed the outskirts of the village Robbie said he thought he had seen a couple of guys who looked like the ABA. Luke didn't see them and assumed that Robbie was making it up. He couldn't imagine Spud or Chucky enjoying a stroll around the village.

When they reached the town, they sauntered along the front, watching the girls eating ice creams, despite it still being a bit chilly. There was a small funfair that was beginning to open up for the weekend crowds, at the far end of the pier and they wandered along it. It was quite noisy, with all the music, and the shrieks from people of all ages. They could smell the candy floss, toffee apples and hot dogs, which made their mouths water. There were some kiddie rides and simple sideshows like hook-a-duck that didn't appeal to them. But there were some quite new rides with names like The Terminator, Armageddon and The Big One.

Unfortunately, apart from the money his mum had given him for his running shoes Luke didn't have any more cash. Robbie only had enough for his lunch and bus fare back to the village. They decided to go and find out how much the shoes would cost so that they could decide if they had anything to spare for a couple of rides on the fair. The shop was pretty easy to find. It sold everything for the outdoors from camping stoves to self-inflating sleeping pads. There was a huge dummy modelling a range of insulated long johns and vests, which they found ridiculous. A young man came over and asked if he could be of assistance.

Luke asked if he could show them where the running shoes were and he took them to the back of the store where a huge array of shoes, boots, trainers and all manner of footwear was displayed. The young man rightly concluded that they would not want the most expensive range, so he pointed out the cheapest pair of spikes in stock. Luke was surprised at the price and asked if he had anything cheaper. Unfortunately, they were ten pounds more than he could afford.

'Can you lend me your lunch money, so that I can afford them? He asked Robbie.

'Nah,' said Robbie.

He was just about to put it back on the shelf when Robbie asked for the other size ten shoe so that he could try them on together for size. The assistant disappeared into the stock room.

Luke said to Robbie, 'What are you doing? You know I can't afford them.'

'Well, it won't hurt to just try them on, will it?' countered Robbie.

As the assistant hovered nearby, Luke sat down on a low seat and tried them on. They fitted perfectly and he was utterly disappointed that he was unable to afford them. He took them off and put his trainers back on. He was determined to go to work at Catherine's shop to earn enough to pay the balance so that he could come back and get them as soon as possible. As he slipped his shoes back on, the assistant headed off to help someone who was creating a huge mound in the middle of the shop, which included saucepans, a stove, a backpack, a water purifier and several small pieces of equipment including a penknife, compass and a nifty helmet inset with a miner's lamp.

Luke and Robbie left the shop and walked back towards the fairground. 'Let's go on The Big One first,' suggested Robbie.

'We haven't got any money, remember? I'm not spending this money; I'm going to save up and get the spikes,' fumed Luke.

Robbie then partly unzipped his jacket and showed Luke the shoes that he had taken as soon as the assistant had turned his back.

'Oh my God, I didn't want you to nick them. We've got to take them back. We might have been caught on

CCTV, and I'm trying to go straight. I've never stolen anything for myself, and I don't want to start now.'

'Don't worry, they didn't have any CCTV, I checked,' Robbie reassured him.

'I don't care. I don't want to keep thieving stuff. I could have got some more money and come back and bought them,' Luke argued.

'Well you didn't steal them; I did. Besides, whenever you stole cigs for Damian, you always gave me some, so I'm just returning the favour. Think of all the punishments you've taken for stealing stuff that wasn't even for you.'

Luke, alternately thrilled to have them and nervous about the fact that they were stolen, shouted, 'we can't take them back now; how could we explain how we walked out without paying for them?'

'Stop going on about it. I'm just relieved they didn't have a security tag in them,' said Robbie.

'What? I hadn't even thought of that. You could have set off an alarm.' Argued Luke.

'But I didn't! Go and take them back if you don't want them,' said Robbie.

Luke was too stressed and embarrassed to return to the shop, so they finally calmed down and called a truce.

They spent the rest of the day on the fairground and caught the bus back to the village, feeling pretty sick from a combination of the rides, fizzy drinks and too much candy floss.

Chapter 38 – The Trap

Most days after school, Luke went up to William's farm for an hour. He was enjoying doing his community service, much more than he would have thought possible. He had learned so much; admittedly none of it would be of much use if they went back to live in the city. Living in the village had been more fun than he imagined, but Damian was already talking about moving back, for some reason, even though the housing development was only beginning to get underway. His mum and Damian had had quite a heated discussion and then they had gone to the pub, so he had no idea how the conversation had finished.

William was waiting for him when he arrived.

'Do you want a cup of tea?' William asked him.

'Yes please,' said Luke.

He'd been trying to remember his manners when he was with William and recently when he'd said thank you to his mum, she had choked on something. He had never really bothered with things like that before, but according to William, people respected you more, not less, for being polite.

They sat down at the table and they both seemed to sense that they had something they wanted to get off their chests. Luke started tentatively with, 'My community service is nearly finished.'

William sighed and said, 'Yes, I know, boyo.'

There was a long awkward silence, and then they both said at the same time, 'I've been thinking.'

'Go on then, after you,' they both said together.

'No, it's alright, you first,' said Luke.

At the risk of being rejected outright, William explained to Luke that if he could help with some of the work on the farm, he would be able to grow a lot more crops and sell them to Catherine or on a stall at the monthly farmers' market. He would be willing to pay; he didn't expect Luke to work for nothing, and he could also take eggs, fruit and vegetables home to his mum.

Luke was overjoyed but wasn't prepared to show it. So he shrugged and said it sounded alright. He listened as William explained that he would like to keep more chickens but that he had been having trouble recently. Something had been getting into the hen house and killing some of the hens and eating all the eggs.

Luke said, 'I've heard about things like that; it's usually foxes, isn't it? We haven't got to go fox hunting, have we? Because I'm not wearing one of those poncy red jackets and I've never ridden a horse!'

William smiled inwardly at the idea of The Master of the Hunt allowing Luke to ride one of his expensive hunters.

'Actually, I don't think it is foxes. I think it might be mink. They're aggressive and I've seen their tracks.'

'I thought they lived near water,' Luke said, surprising himself that he must have listened in one of his lessons and picked up that piece of information.

'They do, but they travel across the land as well. They're destructive and can kill animals larger than themselves. They attack cats and dogs but have no natural predators themselves. That's why they have got so out of hand in the wild.'

'They won't bite us, will they?'

'No, not unless you try to touch one of them.'

'So how do we get rid of them?'

'We need to put down traps all along the riverbank where there's been mink activity. They're fairly distinctive and if we bait the traps with cat food or kippers, we should be able to catch some of them.'

'But won't you get in trouble for trapping them?'

'Not at all. You can trap American mink because they're not native to this country. There used to be loads of water voles around here, which are lovely, gentle, little creatures, but you hardly ever see them now. The mink kill whole families.'

They went down to the riverbank carrying two traps each, and William explained how to spot the signs. Then he showed how to bait and prepare the traps. Luke was quite impressed when William told him that he would shoot any mink caught.

As they were returning to the farm, Luke listened as William explained the plans he had for cultivating the large field and which crops he was planning to grow. On a few occasions recently, Luke had forgotten to be a surly teenager and was full of enthusiasm and it was contagious.

Luke's good mood lasted until he got home. He wanted to tell his mum about the job with William, but as he approached the front door he could hear raised voices.

'Why the hell can't you hold onto a job for more than five minutes?' said Beth.

'It's not my fault. I was working hard up there, but they were always taking the mickey. Giving me the worst jobs and blaming me for losing stock. But why are you so bothered? This is just a one-horse town; we could easily go back home and get jobs there.'

'I don't want to leave. I like it here and Luke is settling in at the school.'

'Well tough. You've got no choice. They won't let you keep the caravan on the site without me, so that's that,' Damian said with finality. 'I'm going down to the pub; I need a pint.' And he left, slamming the caravan door behind him.

Luke felt as though he had been punched in the stomach. He was devastated at the prospect of going back home so soon. The flat didn't even feel like home; this caravan as cramped as it was, felt like home, his first real home and he desperately wanted to stay. The lack of a bedroom was made up for by the feeling of being safe, some new friends who even liked running, learning new skills on the farm and even going to school. As soon as Damian was out of view he opened the door and walked over to his mum.

'I'm sorry love, but we won't be able to stay here any longer. Damian lost his job today, and I don't think he'll find another one around here.'

'But Mum. I can get a job; surely then we'd be able to stay?'

'I doubt there will be much work for you. And you'd only be able to work part-time; it just wouldn't work. I wish it would, but we have to face facts. We have to move back to Manchester.'

'Mum, William has offered me work on his farm, as much as I like. He wants to run it like it used to be and sell the produce at the shop and the farmers' markets. He said that I can bring home fruit and veg as well; surely that would help.'

'I don't think it will make enough of a difference, Luke. I would love to stay here, but we can't without Damian.'

'Please, Mum, will you think about it? I'll leave school right away if I have to,' Luke pleaded.

'No, I don't want you to leave school; we'll both get in trouble, and besides, you seem to be doing well there. Listen, I don't want to get your hopes up. I honestly don't think we will have any alternative, but I will speak to Catherine and see if she can give me more hours or offer some advice. Let's sleep on it and talk about it tomorrow.'

Luke tried to do his homework but couldn't concentrate. Why did Damian have to go and mess everything up when things were going so well? What a useless waste of space. Luke was determined that when he was older, he wouldn't keep letting his family down as the men in his mother's life had. He never really registered that they were the men in his life too.

Chapter 39 – School Field Trip

It was the morning of the school field trip and Luke was feeling sick. There had been a deafening silence between his mum and Damian since the previous evening, and his mum was troubled and distracted at breakfast. Luke had been tossing and turning all night as well, alternately afraid at the prospect of returning to Manchester and elated at the prospect of his mum agreeing to stay, but without Damian. He had even imagined that they could possibly live above the shop with Catherine and her mum.

He made himself a packed lunch and prepared for the trip to Capel Garmon. At least he wouldn't have to sit through a maths lesson trying to understand quadratic equations.

He got on the bus with Robbie, Scott and Joey. He tried to pay attention as Robbie muttered that he was feeling sick. He'd tried to get out of the trip, but his mum had insisted that he go since he had already missed a couple of days at school and she thought the walk in the fresh air would do him good. His asthma seemed to be getting worse and she had expected it to improve once they got out of the city away from all the pollution and traffic. He had spent half an hour trying to find his inhaler. In the end, he had given up the search and pinched Scott's.

'Well, what if Scott needs it?'

'He'll be alright. I don't want to go on this trip; I've only got three cigs to last all day.'

Luke suddenly remembered Robbie's challenge to Mr Edison and the skinny wimps and thought Robbie was trying to find an excuse to get out of exerting himself. Although he'd normally have been excited at the prospect of getting out of school for the day, Luke had too many things on his mind to appreciate it. However, once Joey started talking about it he felt quite enthusiastic.

Joey explained that although it was quite a steep walk, it wasn't long. 'And there's a burial chamber that's over 4,000 years old where Neolithic farmers have been buried. Down at the gorge, there's a lot to see, particularly the waterfalls that thunder down into the Fairy Glen. The wildlife's amazing, with loads of otters and ducklings at this time of year. Further down, there's a pond where there are lots of wading birds like Lapwings and Red Shanks. And the salmon ladder that was built ages ago, which the salmon use to go upstream in August. Oh and a café where you can get white pizza and great apple pie if you're still hungry after your packed lunch.'

'It sounds brilliant, you really know your stuff,' enthused Luke.

'Oh yeah, really great,' said Robbie sarcastically. 'I've always wanted to see a Prehistoric burial thingy and fairies, and salmon climbing a ladder.'

'It's Neolithic you moron,' chided Luke.

'What difference does it make? I still don't want to go,' said Robbie.

'Why not?' asked Joey. 'Surely it's better than studying Shakespeare and Calculus; or are you a bit of a geek?'

'No I'm not a geek, but wandering about the countryside is not my idea of fun.'

'Well don't you think you should try getting used to it, or are you not planning on staying long?' Asked Joey.

That comment made Luke feel sick with anxiety as he recalled the conversation that had taken place the evening before with his mum and his bright mood changed to a dark foreboding.

The bus arrived at school shortly afterwards and they all piled into the playground. Robbie said that he was going for a quick smoke before they had to go to Capel Garmon. Joey, sensing that Luke seemed uneasy, asked if he was alright. 'Yes, I'm fine. I've just got something on my mind.'

'You're not worried about the race the week after next, are you?' Joey joked.

'No, yes; well a bit,' he responded uncertainly.

'James said that you were brilliant the other night, so you must be doing alright,' he tried to reassure him.

'You don't know if Catherine has got a spare room, do you? It's just that we might not be able to stay in the caravan for much longer,' Luke blurted.

Surprised by the change of direction Joey said, 'No, I don't think she has. Her sister Genevieve has just come home. I don't know how long she's thinking of staying, but her mum is ill so she may stay awhile.'

'Oh yes, I think my mum mentioned her. She pinched some vodka.'

'Did she?' Joey looked alarmed.

Luke ran over to the toilets and shouted at Robbie to get a move on as the rest of the class was getting ready to leave. They joined the back of the queue, Robbie dragging his feet all the way. Once Mr Edison had explained exactly the route they were to take and got them into pairs, they set off across the field to Capel Garmon. Luke and Robbie stayed at the back of the group and Luke explained the problem with Damian and why he was so worried.

'Wouldn't you be better off without him? I don't know anyone who likes him – well apart from your mum that is,' he said apologetically.

'Not financially. And if he isn't working on the building site we won't be allowed to stay on the land.'

'I wonder if my dad could arrange something?' Asked Robbie.

'I don't think so. There are only so many points to connect the caravan to and someone else will need ours. I can't see our mums cooperating with each other, can you?

The thought of Beth and Sandra sharing the vital water connection made them both write that idea off as a non-starter.

The trip to Capel Garmon went well. Luke stayed at the back of the group with Robbie who was finding it pretty exhausting. He had to use his inhaler several times, but even Robbie seemed to admire the atmosphere of the place. Sam had used a combination of chair, sticks and being thrown over Kieran's shoulder for the rocky parts. He preferred to take part in as many activities as possible, and in the process made Robbie feel self-conscious about his lack of effort. The group stood at the base of the waterfall then Luke took his turn standing underneath one of the tall trees and looked up. It made him feel weird.

The one aspect that most surprised Luke was some of the tiny stuff on the edge of the pond, such as the mayflies with three tails as well as frogs and insects. He even talked to the whole group about setting the mink traps with William and was surprised at how much animosity everyone felt towards the mink. The only disappointment was Robbie's lack of interest throughout the day.

Chapter 40 – Shoplifting

On his way home from school, Joey popped in to see William. He wanted to ask him how Luke was getting on as he was concerned following their conversation in the morning.

'He seems to be doing well. I'll miss him when he goes.'

'What do you mean?'

'The family may not stay here.'

'What makes you say that?'

'Well he seems like a decent enough lad, but I don't think his mum is trustworthy.'

'How do you know?'

'Just between you and me, Catherine is thinking of sacking his mum. She noticed that a couple of bottles of vodka have gone missing, and some other stuff.'

Joey sucked in his breath and looked embarrassed.

'That might not have been Beth.'

'Well, Catherine said you warned her to keep an eye on Beth and she's grateful to you.'

'Oh no. This is my fault. I feel guilty about speaking out of turn. Apparently, Beth caught Genevieve helping herself.'

'So she's back is she? I thought I caught a glimpse of her the other day but I wasn't sure. She'll be trouble.'

'Should I try and speak to Catherine?'

'Yes, I think you should. Just to set the record straight.'

'I'll go now, see you later.' Joey ran back down to the village and walked into the café.

On the far left-hand side of the café, Catherine had pushed two tables up against the wall and had arranged a computer on each, with a printer in the middle. The printer was the type that could scan, print and photocopy and there was a sign above it with the various prices. Joey wondered which decade the various bits and pieces had been made in. The base units and pieces of equipment looked as if they were manufactured in so many different countries it was like a United Nations' car boot sale.

'Well, I took your advice Joey, and we now have our own internet café.'

'Yes, I can see. Where did you buy all this stuff?'

'Oh, I didn't buy any of it. I put a notice in the window and everyone donated bits and pieces.'

'Really? Does it all work?'

'Well not really. That's where you come in. I thought you could connect up all the wires and sort it all out.'

'I'll try,' he responded less than enthusiastically, whilst thinking that Steve Jobs would struggle to achieve anything worthwhile with the components and Bill Gates would probably find the software challenging.

A couple of hours and several hot chocolates later, Joey had managed to get both computers working and linked up to the printer. However, the internet connections were painfully slow. He mentioned it to Catherine but she thought she should wait and see how popular the computers were before she invested in the highest broadband. However, Joey thought that the computers

204

would prove to be popular if they had the fastest possible connections already. She decided to think about it and make a decision the following day.

'Anyway, I think you should be getting along home now and thank you for all your help, Joey.'

'You're welcome. By the way, can I just have a quick word about Beth?'

'There's no need Joey. I took your advice.'

'Really. And?'

'And I let her go today. But please keep that to yourself.'

'Oh no. It's not because of the vodka is it?'

'What do you know about the vodka Joey?'

Joey blushed and looked at his feet.

'She mentioned to Luke that Genevieve had helped herself to some vodka. Sorry, I don't want you to think badly of your sister when you've only just been reunited.'

'It's hard to think any other way about my sister.'

'Perhaps she just forgot to put the money in the till.'

'Yes, she's got a history of doing that.'

'Oh. So what are you going to do about Beth?'

'I'm going to have to apologise and grovel to her to come back.'

'I'm really sorry. I will apologise to Beth if it helps. I didn't mean to cause all this trouble.'

'That won't be necessary. I don't want her to know we've been discussing her behind her back. But the thing is, some cigarettes have gone missing too, and Genevieve doesn't smoke.'

'Oh.' There was a painful silence whilst Joey absorbed that piece of information. He didn't know what it was that Luke had shoplifted, but he had never seen him smoking.

'There were a couple of strangers a few days ago but they paid for the stuff and they seemed to have plenty of cash. They didn't look like they were from the building site.'

'Were they wearing tracksuits? I think I saw them.'

'Yes, all in black. I'll keep my eye on them if they come back.'

'Well, I'd better be going. Nos dda.'

'Nos dda Joey.'

Chapter 41 – Cable

When Joey got home he found James full of excitement as he was to be allowed to work ten hours per week in the Sales Office, which was due to open shortly.

Joey congratulated him and explained what had happened with Catherine and Beth.

'Well even if Beth is honest, her husband isn't.' said Paul.

'Really? How do you know he isn't?'

'Rhodri and Gavin were convinced he had stolen cables from the site. And he wouldn't own up, they had to search the whole site. It wasted half a day. Then they called the police who made him open up the boot of his car and there they were – several reels of expensive cable.'

'Oh no. What did the police do?'

'They arrested him, but he didn't go quietly. Tried accusing Rhodri of planting the stuff in his car, said he had never touched the stuff.'

'Well, why didn't they take his fingerprints?'

'They probably will. He probably thinks he can run rings around the local police, but they have an excellent record for solving crimes.'

'That wouldn't be because the most dastardly crime that's been committed round here in ages was when someone locked a goat in the police station?' Asked James.

'Has he been sacked?' Joey wanted to know.

'Yes, and not a moment too soon. He was forever causing trouble.'

'Why what else did he do?'

'He turned up without steel toe-capped boots on the first day. He kept taking off his hard hat on site. And he pinched Rhodri's lunch.'

'Of all the people to get on the wrong side of, I wouldn't pick Rhodri.'

'I know. Apparently, he's not just ex-army, he's ex-SAS.'

'Really? I knew he was ex-army because he always says things like sixteen hundred hours, action stations and he always uses the phonetic alphabet. But how do you know he's ex-SAS?'

'Well, he's never actually confirmed it, it's just a rumour, he rarely discusses his military career. But he's incredibly fit, so I wouldn't be at all surprised.'

Chapter 42 – Like a Father

On the evening after Beth had been given her job back job at the café and Damian had been sacked, the three of them were sitting down to their evening meal. Beth served the quiche that she'd brought from the café, with a salad and some baby new potatoes. Unsurprisingly, Damian had something to say about the meal.

'Salad? Where're the chips? I'm sick of all this rubbish.'

'Well, you do yourself chips,' she replied.

They were all surprised. She rarely snapped at Damian, but maybe she was finally learning to stand up for herself. Luke didn't say anything, but he didn't get up and leave the table either.

'Don't you shout at me. Who do you think puts all this food on the table anyway?'

'Well, it certainly isn't you. I brought the quiche home and Luke brought the salad and potatoes from William,' she replied quietly.

'Well, I provide all of the other meals and pay all the bills. You don't think working at that café for minimum wage is paying for all this do you?' He gestured around the room.

'I am not paid minimum wage, actually. And I contribute to the bills, so stop acting the big man.'

'You cheeky bitch,' he bellowed. 'Your contribution is minuscule, so don't kid yourself. You don't earn enough to feed a dog.'

'You don't earn anything at all anymore, do you? No, because you can't hold down a job for five minutes. You're pathetic.'

'Oh, pathetic, am I. You had better watch your mouth or I'll go back home without you.'

'Well, you would be doing us all a favour if you did.' Luke's stomach was churning with anxiety, but he hoped his mum would be strong this time.

Damian sat there dumbfounded. 'And just how will you cope if I go?'

'We'll manage, don't worry about us.'

'I'm not worried. Oh, don't tell me, you've got another fella you're thinking of shacking up with.'

'No, I haven't, but it would be no business of yours if I had, would it?'

'Yes, it would. You're still my wife and you will behave like one. If I say we're going back home, we're going, and you two had better get used to the idea,' he bellowed.

At this point, Luke said, 'We won't get used to the idea, because we're not coming. So why don't you sod off and leave us alone?'

'You cheeky little brat. I have been like a father to you, and that's the way you speak to me?' He then addressed Beth. 'Are you going to let him speak to me like that?'

'Yes. You have indeed been like a father to him, but since his father was utterly useless and vile, that's hardly a good thing, is it? And what he says is true; we're not coming with you.'

Luke could not believe this turn of events. Damian had always, absolutely always, got his own way in the past. When his mum had wanted a church wedding, he had told her that it would be much more relaxed and informal at the register office. When Beth had wanted another child, he had promised that they would have one next year, and it was always next year - then he went and had a vasectomy without telling her. When she had wanted a nippy little Mini that would be easy to park in Manchester, he had persuaded her that they really needed a sporty, ancient Capri. She had never dared to contradict him and he couldn't believe that she had the nerve now.

As Damian stood up, Beth and Luke were startled. 'You will both regret this. I don't like being spoken to like that.'

'Sorry, didn't mean to hurt your feelings,' said Luke sarcastically. 'Would you like a hand with your packing?'

He shouted an expletive and stormed out of the room. They could hear him moving about in the tiny bedroom.

'What are we going to do now, Mum?' asked Luke quietly.

'Well, my mum owns the caravan so he can't kick us out, but with the toilet and shower arrangements, we need to be able to hook up to a water supply and some kind of drain or sewer. If we can't arrange that we'll have to go back to the old flat, at least it's not sold yet.'

At that point, Damian came back in with both of the big suitcases filled with his belongings. He then picked up the portable television and placed it in a black bin bag. He shouted to them, 'Don't think you can come grovelling back to me when everything goes pear-shaped here.' Then he slammed the door so hard that most of the neighbours must have heard it.

Beth ran to the door to make sure that it was alright and then locked it from the inside. Luke bolted into the bedroom to see if he'd taken anything of theirs. He hadn't, but he'd left a mess in the bathroom.

As he'd removed his toiletries from the bathroom cabinet, he had knocked over a bottle of Luke's hair gel. Since the lid wasn't on it properly, it had spilt onto the edge of the wash-hand basin and was dripping down onto the bath mat. In the bedroom, he had knocked over a bottle of Beth's perfume and it was making a mess on the dressing table and the carpet. And when he had removed the television, he had smashed her little china ornament. It wasn't expensive, but her mum had given it to her for her eighteenth birthday.

As Beth cleared up the mess, Luke checked in the kitchen cupboards to see if they had anything to celebrate with. There wasn't much, so he made pancakes and added a pile of strawberries. They sat down together and as they ate them; Luke told his mum all about the trip to Capel Garmon. She couldn't believe that Robbie had been so enthusiastic that he had even asked questions about birds – it was amazing. The birds in question were ospreys, and the young males were pretty lazy when it came to building nests, so they often used old ones, regardless of what condition they were in. She commented that the same attitude extended to humans sometimes.

Chapter 43 – The Job

Joey was enjoying the rush of the cool air on his face as he cycled down to the village on his mountain bike. He decided that since he couldn't take part in the race he might as well find his trusty bike. As he neared the chapel, he spotted Luke scrubbing paint off the wall. He cycled in through the gate and pulled up with a scattering of gravel behind Luke. Luke seemed surprised.

'I didn't do this.' Luke was trying to look innocent but came across as defensive.

'So why are you cleaning it off then?'

'Because I'll be blamed. I'm still doing my community service.'

'Well, why not make Robbie clean it?'

'Why do you assume it was Robbie?'

'No one from here would do such a thing on an ancient building. We might think the chapel is boring but we wouldn't be so disrespectful. Not even Tommo.'

'It's only an old church.' Said Luke.

'When my mum died this is where they held her funeral.'

'Oh sorry, I didn't think.'

'It's alright, it was a few years ago, but I still miss her. Everyone liked her.'

They both felt a moment of awkwardness and were quiet for a few minutes.

'I wonder if those thugs who have been hanging around would do it.'

'That's not likely. If they are from the ABA their graffiti is way above this crap. And you're right, it was Robbie. I recognise the blue paint. He once caused Scott to get beaten up because of his graffiti.'

'Why does he do it?'

'I think he thinks he's talented, but street art follows trends and his style isn't appreciated.'

'And is he?'

'Well when our art teacher heard him boasting that he would one day be the best artist in the country, Mr Brown said, "You're not even the best artist in this class".'

'So, again, why don't you make him clean it?'

'Because he wouldn't. And he would just deny it was him.'

Joey could see Luke was struggling so he started at the other end and they worked towards the middle until it was all gone. It left a really clean patch in the middle of the dirty old stone, but that couldn't be helped.

'I'm supposed to start working in the shop with my mum and I'm going to be late. Would you take the bucket and brushes back to my caravan on your way back?'

'Yes, just leave it here for now and I'll pick it up on the way back. I need to buy some stuff for breakfast, I'll come with you.'

Luke felt a bit self-conscious as he entered the shop, particularly as Catherine seemed a bit wary when he arrived. She asked him to bring some heavy boxes from the storeroom and start stocking up the shelves. As he got to work Joey asked Catherine how the internet service was going.

'Really well. I'm quite surprised. And I've increased the bandwidth to one megabyte. That's huge that is!'

Joey smiled, paid for the food and left.

As Paul prepared breakfast for them Joey told them what had happened with Luke.

'Well, it is his fault this time. He may not have had much say in choosing his stepfather, but he can choose his friends. I'm not sure he's someone you two should be spending so much time with him.'

Joey wandered outside, mulling over the comment. He thought Luke should spend more time with himself and James, as they would be a positive influence and help him settle down in the village.

Over in the distance, he could see someone walking up the lane. They were nearly bent double with the exertion. As they stood upright to light a cigarette, Joey recognised Robbie and wondered what he was doing. Robbie went to the patch of the wall that Luke had repaired and tried to push the section over. It didn't budge, even after he kicked it. He pushed it nearer to the top, but it still held firm. There were at least thirty sheep in the field and Joey wondered what would happen if Robbie managed to break a hole in the wall.

It was then Joey spotted William coming down from the hill with his sheepdog, Dylan, rounding up some of his hardier flock of sheep from the highest part of the hill. William noticed Robbie trying to dismantle the wall. He watched Robbie kicking and shoving the wall for several minutes without success. At that point, Robbie climbed

215

over the wall into the field and managed to dislodge a couple of the smaller stones. He threw them at one of the sheep that was getting close to him.

Joey didn't know what to do. So he watched as William hid behind one of the trees in the field and whistled to Dylan to herd all the sheep over to Robbie. Initially, Robbie was quite aggressive, kicking out at the sheep as they neared him. However, as the ones at the back pushed the rest forward, he was soon surrounded by them. He tried pushing them away with his hands and shouting at them, but they persisted in coming forward.

When they continued past Robbie, William whistled to Dylan to turn them back. He continued to hide behind the tree, giving commands by whistling, and as Robbie had his earbuds in, he couldn't hear the whistles.

The sheep gradually herded Robbie towards the corner of the field near the gate. It was also the area that got trampled on the most, and as it was in a dip, huge amounts of water were collected there and created a boggy area. Robbie slipped and slithered his way across this patch and, just as he nearly made it to the gate, the sheep changed direction again and he fell headlong into the mud. The sheep walked around him and stood huddled in the area whilst Dylan stood nearby waiting for the next command. Robbie got to his feet and ran to the gate and leapt over it. It was the most athletic thing William and Joey had ever witnessed him doing and were both pleasantly surprised.

Robbie ran back down the hill, checking over his shoulder, as though he believed that the sheep had the potential to leap the wall and chase after him. William

216

laughed so hard that he had to sit down under the tree to catch his breath.

Chapter 44 – The Tractor

Luke couldn't believe how different his life felt now that Damian had gone. He couldn't credit how much impact one person could make on his life. The last week or so had been great. His first day at the shop had gone smoothly, despite the initial rocky start. He had stocked up all the shelves; priced everything up; rearranged the stock in the storeroom so that it was easier to access; and got rid of a couple of huge spiders.

When a customer complained about the speed of the internet access he suggested moving everything over to the window to get the best possible signal. Catherine was a bit dubious but he demonstrated with his mobile that he could get a stronger signal there, compared to where the back of the café. She had let him move both computers and was surprised by the result. He had then deleted a lot of the old programmes and files from the computers and installed some de-fragging software which speeded things up even further.

As soon as Robbie came in Luke took his break so that Catherine wouldn't think he was skiving. They joined the queue behind Fred, who ordered Welsh rarebit.

When they were served they sat near Fred. He seemed to be pushing his food around his plate, and when he caught Robbie watching he offered it to him.

'Why what's wrong with it?'

'Nothing, it's just cheese on toast.'

'So why did you order it, if you don't like it.'

'I wasn't sure what it was when I ordered it.'

'And don't you like cheese on toast.'

'Well, it has extra ingredients.'

'Such as?'

'Mustard.'

'Oh.'

'And Worcestershire sauce.'

'Yeah?'

'I don't like mustard or Worcestershire sauce.'

'Well just leave it.'

'I can't. I don't want Catherine to think I don't like her cooking.'

'She probably won't take it personally.'

'She might. I think she likes me.'

'What makes you think that?'

'When I run past every day, she always smiles at me.'

Luke thought it was probably more like a smirk but didn't say so, after all his white shorts had been a source of amusement for him on a couple of occasions.

He finished his lunch and went to work behind the counter in the shop so that his mum could take her break. Robbie followed him through and asked for a packet of his favourite cigarettes. Knowing that he had taken a packet before without paying for them, Luke put them on the counter and told Robbie that he had to pay for them. However, he just put them in the pocket of his tracksuit, thanked Luke and walked out. Luke shouted after him, but Robbie ignored him and carried on. There was a customer in the shop, so Luke had to wait and serve her. As soon as she left he ran to the door to try and catch

Robbie, but there was no sign of him. Luke was checking through his pockets to see if he had enough money to put in the till when Catherine came through.

'Are you alright love?'

'Yes, I'm fine thanks.'

Just as he was about to open the till and put the money in, she returned, so he quickly closed it again. He was busy on and off for most of the afternoon and completely forgot to pay for Robbie's cigarettes.

After he had finished work, Luke went for another run. His training with James was going well. They were counting down to the race and it was only a week away now. He had always managed to keep up with James, but he wasn't sure if James was giving it his all or was merely cruising.

The only fly in the ointment was the uncertainty regarding the caravan. His mum was going to ask a local councillor if there was any other land in the village they could park on, or possibly a caravan park in the immediate area. It would have to be close by as they had no form of transport now that Damian had taken the car.

When he returned from his run his mum told him how the conversation with Reg had gone.

'He was horrible to me. He said the caravan was an eyesore and that it would put tourists off and even suggested it might attract gypsies to the area.'

'What a cheek. It's not even old. What did you say to him?'

'I was so shocked I couldn't think of anything to say at the time. Then he dared to suggest I buy one of the new houses.'

'As if.'

'I don't know what we can do now. I'm sorry love, I know you're disappointed.'

'I really don't want to go back to Manchester yet. What about asking William? He's got loads of land.'

'We don't know him well enough.'

'But he might be our only option.'

'Why do I always have to feel so desperate?'

'It's not that bad. Stop over-reacting. Just go and talk to William.'

'Apart from the odd occasion when I've served him in the shop, I've never spoken to him.'

'Well, he usually has a drink on a Saturday night. You could go to the pub and speak to him.'

They mulled things over and then decided to ask William the following day. They thought it would be unfair to tackle him after he had had a drink, so they decided that Luke would go to work on the farm as usual on Sunday and his mum could come and meet him after she had finished work.

Luke got up early on Sunday and ran up to the farm. He listened as William explained his plans in detail and then went on to tell him about using the tractor. Luke was keen, so they went out to the field where it was standing. William gave Luke a thorough health and safety briefing and showed him where all the various attachments went. Then Luke sat beside William as he drove the tractor the

221

length of the field. It was a bit bumpy, but it didn't seem to concern Luke at all. He seemed to be thoroughly enjoying himself.

They ploughed the entire field to a fine tilth, which took several hours. The tractor was quite noisy so they didn't get much opportunity to talk, but when they went inside for something to eat, William explained the various crops that he intended to grow. He was going to divide the field nearest to the farmhouse into sections and grow root vegetables, salad vegetables and potatoes. He was also going to grow several items in the greenhouses, such as tomatoes and cucumbers.

William hardly paused for breath as he explained the type of compost he would use to improve the quality of the soil. Worm-cast compost was a favourite, as he could produce some of it himself. He told Luke in detail about the worms that ate household waste like potato peelings, and the end product was the compost.

Luke blurted, 'you mean it's worm err worm …?'

'Droppings?' said William politely. 'Yes, it's like the circle of life all over again.'

Luke was trying to weigh up if it would be preferable to have food that was fertilized by dead lions rather than the excrement of worms.

Luke had been wondering how to mention the subject of Damian's arrest but didn't know if William wanted to ignore the matter. But after a short silence, it all came pouring out. How difficult life had been for himself and his mum, how demanding and nasty Damian could be and how Luke had been stealing cigarettes for him for years, to his shame. He even explained that after days of soul searching, his mum had decided that she didn't want anything more to do with him. However, Luke was mortified to admit, that it left them in a difficult position in terms of where they would live.

William felt upset and disappointed for them and asked if they had decided to stay in the village or return to the city.

'Well, we would love to stay here. The school is alright, but don't tell Robbie I said that will you? He'll roast me.'

'Don't worry, I won't say anything.'

'And my mum likes working for Catherine. She's learned to cook decent food now; not that she couldn't cook before; but it was mostly packet stuff, you know. We know the difference now. And it's the race next week; I can't wait. I just wish I had some idea of how good I am compared to everyone else. I can't tell whether James is trying or if he's going slowly so that I can keep up with him.'

'Well, you'll know soon enough how good you are.'

'I don't think Lloyd Morgan will risk cheating, do you?'

'He may do. I haven't had any dealings with him personally, but I've heard quite a lot about him and his father. They sound like a pair of rogues, to be honest, his father went to prison for credit card fraud, and there have been rumours about Lloyd causing trouble, so keep your eye on him.'

They seemed to have gone completely off track with the conversation, and Luke was wondering how to steer it back to the fact that he and his mum would be imminently homeless. Just as he was thinking of how to change the subject back, there was a light knock on the door.

William opened the door and found Beth standing there. They both started to apologise at the same time – William, for keeping Luke so long, and Beth, for popping around unannounced.

'Come in, come in,' said William. 'Would you like a cup of tea or do you have to dash off?'

'A cup of tea would be nice, thanks.'

As he put the kettle on, they sat awkwardly.

'Luke tells me that you've had a bit of bad luck lately. I hope you don't mind him mentioning it to me,' said William as he brought the cups and teapot to the table.

'Not at all,' she replied. She hoped Luke would explain which piece of bad luck he was referring to. There had been so many trials and tribulations, but would he consider Damian being arrested and then leaving them as bad luck?

'He says that you need to park the caravan somewhere.'

'Yes, that's right,' she replied.

'Well, there's plenty of room in the farmyard.'

'Would you consider allowing us to move the caravan there?'

'Of course. I'm not sure it will be ideal during winter though. It can get bleak up here.'

'Well by then I hope to have sold the flat in Manchester, so we may be able to afford to rent somewhere.'

'Well, that's settled then.'

'The problem is that Damian has taken the car back to Manchester, so we have no way of moving the caravan.'

'Well it'll be undignified, but I can tow it with my tractor.'

'Oh, thank you so much.'

'You're welcome. And Luke has been a huge help around here.'

'Luke is keen to work on the farm,' she enthused.

At this, Luke raised his eyebrows. It was all very well being keen to work, but what teenage boy in his right mind admitted to it?

'And I will help out as much as you like. Perhaps you could suggest some jobs that you wouldn't mind me doing so that I don't do anything that you would prefer for me to leave alone.'

'Well, emptying the septic tank is a difficult job.' However, he said this with such a straight face that Beth thought he was serious.

'The septic tank?' she asked. Luke and Beth were both thinking 'Is that what I think it is?' but luckily didn't vocalise the question.

'I'm only kidding. Sorry. I haven't actually got a septic tank. Fred next door has one, and I did mention to him a few times last year to remember to get it emptied.'

'And did he?' asked Luke

'No, not until it was too late.'

'What happened?'

'There was the most God-awful smell. You could smell it even down in the village. I thought someone was going to kill him. Not only was it bad for the environment, but once the sludge overflowed, it damaged the piping and the leach field. It cost him a bloody fortune to get it repaired.'

'Thank goodness you haven't got one then,' said Beth.

They agreed on a moving date and shook hands. Beth and Luke nearly ran all the way home.

Chapter 45 – The Race

It was the morning of the race, and James seemed to be alternately excited, then terrified. Joey was quite envious, but he and his dad were going to go along and keep an eye on things. Joey was going to be at the footbridge and Paul was going to hide near the pass, which led directly to the village and was the alternative route that you could take as a shortcut if you were going to cheat. They didn't want a huge confrontation about it being their word against someone else's, so they had a cunning plan.

When they got down to the registration desk, several runners were milling about. There was a lot of nervous tension in the air. Several of the runners were changing into their running shoes, filling water bottles and limbering up. All the runners had to fill in a form and were given a number on a big sticker that they had to wear. They were shown a picture of the route with an explanation of where the marshals would be standing and where drinks of water would be available. Several first-aiders would be positioned along the route. Anyone who was having any difficulty at all was advised to leave the race immediately.

Lloyd Morgan was at the front of the queue, and his father, Huw, was distributing the runners' numbers. 'See, you're number one already, boyo. Just make sure you come in first place like your old man last year,' he boasted.

By the time James joined the queue to register, several more runners had turned up. Joey was counting out the numbers to work out which would be James'. 'Oh no, you're number thirteen, James, I hope that's not a bad omen,' said Joey.

'I'm not superstitious,' replied James, trying to sound as calm and unflustered as possible. Then he bent down to fasten his shoelace, which looked as though it was already fine to Joey and gestured to the young man behind him to go ahead.

'Nice one,' mumbled Joey.

As he reached the front, Huw said to James 'Oh, now don't go getting all bitter and twisted when you lose. Your old man was a sore loser last time.'

'I won't,' said James enigmatically, grabbing his number and striding away with Joey.

A few more runners registered, including a couple of the men from the building site. Then Fred came along. He was wearing a green t-shirt with the red Welsh dragon emblazoned on the front. He had changed the white satin shorts for bright green lycra, which were presumably easier to run in, but rather less easy on the eye. He seemed very excitable and was chatting animatedly with anyone who would listen.

Luke was number twenty-five and as he was handed his number, Huw said loudly, 'I believe you've recently moved into Rowan.'

'That's right,' confirmed Luke.

'I believe your record is second to none – your criminal record that is. Luckily, we haven't got any of your type in

Llugwy.' Huw and Lloyd high-fived each other. Luke was lost for words. James and Joey were disgusted with Huw and Lloyd and the three of them walked over to the starting line.

'I hope Lloyd doesn't win,' said Luke.

Joey said, 'If Lloyd finishes first, it will be because he's done it fair and square. He won't be able to cheat this time.' Luke wanted to know how he could be sure, but there wasn't time to ask. His mum had popped out of the shop to wave to him, and he could see Catherine and her sister Genevieve behind her. They seemed to be having a pretty heated discussion about something, but he didn't have time to think about them now. He was determined to focus, give this race his full attention and block everything else from his mind. Even though there was only a small prize, the race somehow felt like an important opportunity for him.

The runners, aged from sixteen to sixty, spread out behind a rope, and they were to start running as soon as the starter's gun went off. As Lloyd was standing beside James, he dug him in the ribs and muttered, 'Are you going to donate those shoes to the museum after the race? They're ancient.'

'I'll still be able to outrun you in them,' James responded.

'Don't be absurd, you ridiculous little oik,' sneered Lloyd.

James started to respond, but the starter called to them all to get ready. Instead, he turned to Luke and they wished each other good luck.

The race was to start at the base of the first hill. The first mile or so was quite gravelly and soon the runners were spreading out. Gavin was at the front with Rhodri and a couple of the builders behind them. Luke felt a bit self-conscious running beside James, so he fell into step behind him. He couldn't see Lloyd so assumed he was still behind him. This made Luke uneasy as he considered William's remark the day before not to turn his back on him. But as he had to watch every step, he couldn't turn round to locate him.

The path soon changed from gravel to grass and, as it had been raining a lot in the last day or two, it was quite slippery. Luke was glad that he had his new spikes on. He'd been wearing them every night for a few weeks now, and they were nice and comfortable. This was the easiest part of the course, and everyone was running at a good pace. Soon though, the path dipped up and down alarmingly in places, and some of the slower runners at the back were spreading out a bit.

The course then took them downhill. Most of it was fairly gradual, but there were a couple of parts where it was a bit of a scrabble, and many of the runners steadied themselves with their hands, grabbing tufts of grass as they leapt and ran over some of the rougher parts. As it went uphill one of the runners towards the back lost his balance and as he slipped back down the path, he knocked Fred over. They both had a few nasty scratches but managed to get back on their feet and continue the race.

Then they were in the stream. Everybody was more or less holding onto their position as it was quite difficult

230

negotiating around the rocks. The water was freezing, and as each of them entered the stream, they gasped at the cold. When they finally left the stream, they had to run across three fields, slowing down to climb over a stile and pass through the gate. A few of them swung over the top of the gate rather than pass single file through the small gap.

One of the fields contained William's sheep, and Luke smiled as he remembered Robbie coming into the shop and complaining about how aggressive they were. As they ran past the farmhouse, William shouted encouragement to James and Luke. They were both so breathless that they barely acknowledged him.

Gavin was still in the front scrambling up the hill with Rhodri close on his heels. The two builders were struggling a bit, allowing James and Luke to almost catch up to them. A couple of the other runners were now coming up on their outside, elbows flying, vying for position. He hadn't experienced this much-unexpected aggression in a race since he took part in one against some pupils from a local Catholic school in Manchester. A few months previously, Luke would have just taken it, but as he watched James giving as good as he got, he let his elbow swing into the ribs of the newcomer, and as he did so he realised that it was Lloyd.

As Lloyd nimbly jumped in front of Luke, he deliberately kicked up the stones underfoot so that they hit Luke in the shins. They didn't hurt much but he wanted to show that he was not intimidated. Realising that the bend was up ahead, Luke drew on his reserves of strength and

231

pulled in front of Lloyd. As he reached the bend, the lowest branch from the tree was swinging towards him and he instinctively grabbed it. As he got past it, he let it go and it thought it might have accidentally hit Lloyd in the face. It wasn't a heavy branch, but it would still be an unpleasant surprise.

Luke was surprised that Lloyd didn't make a comeback and try and spoil his chances over the last section, and as he quickly glanced behind him, he couldn't see him at all. Luke was concerned that he might be disqualified if it turned out that he had seriously hurt Lloyd, even accidentally.

Up ahead he could see James, right on the heels of Gavin and Rhodri, and only twenty yards were separating them all. As they ran down the final hill, both James and Luke overtook the builders and approached the footbridge. Huw was the marshal and he stood with his hands on his hips. Joey shouted that no one was ahead of them. But Huw shouted that Lloyd was in front.

He turned to Joey and said, 'You must have missed him when you were playing with your mobile phone.'

'I wasn't playing, I wanted to record the race, so Scott lent it to me.' He then carefully placed Scott's phone in his pocket.

'You should have stood at the finishing line. That way you could have filmed the winner.'

'I have filmed the winner,' he responded. 'I've had the camera running from the sound of the starter's gun. The acoustics on Scott's phone are amazing; they can pick up the sound from here. And it's got the date and time on it.

232

Every runner has to pass over this bridge to prove they've completed the entire course.'

Huw looked a bit ill. He snatched the mobile from Joey's hand. It looked just like an old mobile phone, but he threw it on the floor and smashed it with his heel.

'You need permission to film people. And I'm sure you haven't got the authority.' He shouted at Joey.

'That's no reason to smash my mobile,' responded Joey hotly.

'You said it wasn't yours. You said it was Scott's.'

'This is Scott's,' he said as he held up a sophisticated item from his pocket. 'That was my old phone. Can't you tell the difference between an android and the latest generation smartphone?' Then he turned and ran as fast as he could.

Joey was running back towards the village. He knew Huw was pretty fit but felt sure he would be able to outrun him. Unfortunately, it looked as if Huw had the same thought as he jumped in his jeep, which was parked nearby, and raced after him. Joey was a bit anxious as Huw overtook him and swung his jeep across his path. He slammed his brakes on hard and jumped out of the cab. As he approached, Joey considered running back the way he had come. But Huw held up his hands and asked if he could have a word with him. Joey was a bit nervous but agreed to listen.

Huw pulled him to one side and said, 'Look here's one hundred pounds. You delete the video and we're quits, alright?'

'Alright,' said Joey, deleting the video from Scott's 'phone without hesitation. He took the money and headed back down to the village.

As James and Luke ran the final section to the finishing line, they were neck and neck, with Rhodri close behind them. They had missed the confrontation taking place behind them. Luke felt more excitement than he could recall ever feeling before. He wished he could have beaten James but had used every last ounce of energy to keep up with him.

Luke's mum came up to congratulate them both, and William joined them. 'Well done, both of you. That was so close that I don't think they can separate which one of you was second and which one was third.'

'What do you mean second and third? We should have won!' they shouted.

The umpire came and told them that it was a dead heat and that they were joint second place. Beth was saying to them, 'Joint second; that's fantastic.' She couldn't understand why they weren't congratulating themselves.

All of the other runners finished the race, many of them breaking their own personal records. It had been a tough race, and they were all praising each other and patting one another on the back. Fred was pleased when he realised that Catherine was the first aider. He wanted to remove his top so that she could get to the grazes on the upper part of his arm, but she didn't think that was necessary.

Huw was holding Lloyd's arm aloft and braying about how well his son had done. James and Luke couldn't believe it. They were expecting to be told that they were joint first place. They were breathlessly deliberating over how Lloyd could have overtaken them. They were trying to work out where it could have happened in the confusion around the course, and the last time they could remember seeing him was as they rounded the bend near the low-hanging tree.

Lloyd came over to them and said, 'Perhaps it's time to hang up your boots. Well done anyway; you should be proud of yourselves,' he added patronisingly.

Luke was so angry that he wanted to punch Lloyd. Just then Paul and Joey arrived. Paul approached the judge and said that he would like a word with him. They went to a quiet area.

Joey congratulated them both, asking how they were going to split the prize money.

Lloyd interjected with, 'What prize money, moron? You don't get anything for coming in second, you know!'

Joey responded that they would be sharing the first-place prize money.

James and Luke were puzzled.

Just then the judge announced that there seemed to have been an anomaly and that Lloyd hadn't completed the entire course, so he was being disqualified.

Lloyd looked at his father in utter shock.

'He did complete the final section, I was the marshall and I can vouch for him,' said Huw.

'Well, perhaps you can explain this then.' He held up his mobile phone.

He played a video of the bridge, which showed the time as noon, and the sound of the starter's gun could be heard clearly in the background. He fast-forwarded to nearly an hour later, which was the minimum time it would take to get to the bridge. They stood around watching the video, and the first person to cross the bridge was James, followed by Luke.

As everyone was intently watching the video, Huw grabbed Joey's arm and hissed into his ear, 'You said you were going to delete the video.'

'I did,' said Joey sweetly. 'But I'd already sent a copy of it by WhatsApp and email to my dad. He picked it up from Catherine's internet café. Don't you know anything about technology?'

'I want my money back.'

'What money?' Demanded Paul.

'He gave me a hundred pounds to delete the video of the race,' said Joey, who could manage to appear innocent and cheeky at the same time.

Paul was itching to say something to Huw, but Rhodri held him back. 'Let the police handle it, Paul.'

PC Barry stepped up and said that if it was alright with Paul, he would like to keep hold of the evidence in case criminal charges were brought.

'But we haven't broken the law,' said Huw.

'Let me see. Threatening a minor, fraudulently claiming the prize money, bribery,' listed PC Barry. 'Your rap sheep will be as long as my arm by the time I've finished.'

'Don't be ridiculous,' said Huw.

236

'I can assure you, sir, that these are serious charges. I require you both to come with me to the station where the matter will be dealt with. I do have to warn you, the food's not up to the usual 5-star cuisine you're used to.'

'We don't expect to be there long enough to partake of your food and drink!'

'Well, I suggest you cooperate with me and don't waste police time.'

There were a few sniggers and heckles about Huw doing time and embarrassing himself for the sake of a local race.

Everyone stood around discussing the matter whilst Huw and Lloyd went to the station with PC Barry.

Joey said, 'I feel a bit bad taking the money from him. But he did smash my old mobile; at least now I'll be able to put the money towards a decent one like Scott's. And maybe I could put it on my Christmas present list, Dad?'

Chapter 46 – The Celebration

At breakfast the next day James was telling Joey and his dad about his job in the Sales office. The Sales Manager, Ravi, his wife Tanya and their two children would be moving to the village when their house was built. They had chosen a neat, detached house with a double garage. In the meantime, Ravi would make the commute from Liverpool most days, and stay in local B&Bs a couple of days a week.

Joey, along with James and their dad, had decided to walk to the pub to celebrate James' and Luke's success in the race.

At the pub, they were greeted heartily by everyone, and James received lots of praise. They found Luke and his mum having lunch with William. Pulling a couple of tables together, they joined them.

Shortly afterwards Gavin and Rhodri entered the pub and ordered drinks. Noticing the group in the corner they took their drinks over and joined them.

'Have you recovered from the race yet?' Asked James.

'No! My legs are killing me. I can't work out whether it hurts most when I sit, stand or lie down,' stated Luke.

'Oh, has it put you off running then?' Interrupted Joey.

'No, in fact, it's made me more determined than ever to do the Manchester half-marathon. That's the event I was training for before we came here.'

'When is it? How old do you have to be?' Joey wanted to know.

'It's next month, but I don't think you'll be old enough yet Joey.'

Possibly out of bravado, James, Gavin and Rhodri agreed that they would all enter. They seemed to think running in the city would be much easier than running up and down hills and that city people were generally 'soft'.

Luke was enthusiastic. 'It's a fantastic run, people come from all over the world to take part, and Mo is the favourite to win.'

'Who?' James and Joey asked at the same time.

'Mo Farah. He's a marathon runner originally from Somalia. I've got his book if you want to borrow it.'

James said he'd like to read it, but Joey muttered that he didn't really like reading.

'I don't like reading, but I've read his book twice. Just try it,' said Luke.

'I'm okay, thanks anyway.' Turning away from the rest of the group Joey spoke quietly to Luke. 'James and I need to go and check out some plants if you want to come with us.'

'Plants? What kind of plants?' Luke wanted to know.

'Tommo has been cultivating some cannabis plants in William's old shed.' Said Joey.

'Who's Tommo?' Luke wanted to know.

'The young lad who shuffles about and he's usually wearing James' red hoody,' said Joey.

'Oh yeah, I know who you mean. How many can he grow in that shed?' Asked Luke

'Quite a few. He grows them in small pots then puts them outside when they reach a few inches,' said James.

'I thought cannabis plants had to be grown indoors.' Said Luke.

'Some types are suited to colder climates. He's kept them in pots I think, so he can just lift them back inside if there's a frost.' Said James.

'What are you going to do about them?' Asked Luke.

'We've tried killing some of them with vinegar and washing up liquid, but it doesn't seem to have made much difference. Have you got any suggestions?' Asked James.

'Can't you just set fire to them? It's what the police do when they destroy plants they've seized in Manchester.' Said Luke.

'The outside ones will be damp so without an accelerant it would be difficult. The ones inside would be hard to get to as Tommo practically lives in the shed and one or two tough-looking guys from out of town hang around from time to time.' Said James.

'It's a pity we can't just burn down the shed,' suggested Luke.

'I know. But even though William doesn't use it, lots of hill-walkers do, particularly when it gets a bit warmer,' said James.

'We could keep an eye on the place and as soon as they leave, we could throw all the plants into a pile and set them on fire,' suggested Joey.

'Keep your voice down. Let's go outside and talk,' said James.

They made their excuses to everyone and quickly left the pub. They wandered over to the edge of the field where they could see the shed in the distance.

'We would still need an accelerant. It would be difficult to buy petrol round here,' said James.

'I could get a tin of lighter fuel from the shop. I'll put the money in the till and take it when Catherine's not looking,' said Luke.

'Fantastic. We need to find out when he is most likely to leave the shed,' said James.

'Tommo has to buy food and he usually comes into the shop on Sundays when Catherine sells stuff off like bread.'

'Right, you get the lighter fuel as soon as possible, so we can do the rest,' said James.

'I'm glad to help. Robbo said he saw a couple of guys who looked like some drug dealers from back home. I thought he was joking. You need to be careful; they don't mess around.' Said Luke.

'Well, if you're working next Saturday, get the lighter fuel and give it to us. Then work on Sunday as usual and Whatsapp us as soon as Tommo turns up. We'll burn as much stuff as possible then go and visit William in case he sees the fire and thinks of trying to put it out,' said James.

Luke squinted in the direction of the shed and recognised a couple of the members of the ABA smoking. Their main distinguishing features were their afro fade and red floppy hair. His heart raced.

'Let's go to mine,' he said as he pulled up the collar of his jacket. 'That's Travis and Chucky. The ABA must be running county lines in the area.'

'That's when gangs in cities use kids in rural areas to distribute for them, isn't it?' Asked James.

'Yes, and there's likely to be less competition in places like this. The ABA was constantly involved in fights to protect their turf around Ardwick. The leader, Spud, even beat up Scott just because he thought he'd been damaging his street art,' said Luke.

'What? Why?' Asked James.

'It was a massive mural dedicated to Man United and someone kept spraying over it in blue and changing it to Man City. He even attacked Robbie. I don't know what he did to him, but it must have been serious as he's been a lot more subdued since it happened.'

Now that Damian had left, Luke felt comfortable asking if they wanted to go to his place for a bit. Approaching his caravan just inside William's yard, they wandered over and plonked themselves down on the settee that converted to Luke's bed. They firmed up the plan for the following Sunday that they hoped might make Tommo return to his own home and make the ABA move on.

Chapter 47 – Technology versus Knowledge

During a geography lesson with Mr Edison, Robbie was asked how he would navigate from one place to another if necessary. Robbie said that he would use satellite navigation. Mr Edison asked Robbie what he would do if he didn't have a satellite navigator.

'Well, then I would use my mobile phone and ring someone. I would explain where I was and where I wanted to go.'

'Suppose you couldn't get a signal on your mobile phone?'

'I would send a text. A text often gets through when a call won't.'

'Is that so? I didn't know that. You've taught us something; I'm impressed. And how do you suppose they would work out the route?'

Robbie was looking pleased with himself and replied, 'they would do a request for a route via the AA or Route Planner.'

'What if the directions were too complicated to fit in a text message?'

'I would ask them to send an email via my iPhone.'

'Perhaps we could discuss this in our next IT lesson. In the meantime, trying to leave aside technology just for a moment and assuming your phone was dead, how would you get from one place to another?'

'It would depend on where I was. If I wanted to go from one city to another, there are loads of types of public

243

transport that I could use such as buses, trains, trams, taxis, planes or even a canal barge. I would never dream of thumbing a lift in the city, but if I wanted to go to Llugwy from Rowan, I could flag down a passing car. That's because even if the driver wasn't going to Llugwy, the people around here are so helpful that they would still take me, free of charge, all the way there. Nobody back home would believe that, but it's true.'

The rest of the class laughed at his audacity.

'And why wouldn't you thumb a lift in a big city where there are far more cars available?'

'Because you really would be taken for a ride and you'd be lucky to get out without being mugged, murdered or worse.'

'What could possibly be worse than being murdered?' Someone in the class muttered, aghast.

'You could get your Sat Nav stolen,' he replied cheekily. 'It must happen a lot around here because nobody seems to have one.'

'That's because we use orienteering skills to work out where we are and to determine where we want to go, taking into consideration all of the conditions and features around us. For our next geography lesson, we are going on a field trip. I want you to split up into two groups; you will be left a couple of miles from school and, using only a map, a compass and some common sense, you will navigate your way back. The first team back wins and there are prizes to be won,' he said, waving a couple of large chocolate bars in front of the class.

'Do we all have to go?' asked Robbie.

'Yes, and to show how much faith I have in you, you can be one of the team leaders and Luke can be the other.'

The rest of the pupils seemed quite happy at the prospect of getting out of class for the morning, although they didn't seem confident that either one of them would make a particularly good team leader.

When they got outside for their next break, Luke and Robbie sat on the playground wall and discussed the orienteering trip.

'I don't see why we have to do this. We never had to do any of this at our old school.'

'What's up? Are you afraid I'll beat you?'

'No chance!'

'Well, what's your problem then?'

'I just hate this place. There's nothing about it that I like.'

'I thought you hated Manchester. What exactly are you missing?'

'Loads of stuff. Even the school.'

'What do you miss about our old school?'

'The girls.'

'There are girls here.'

'Yes but they're not like the girls back home. They don't seem to take us seriously.'

'I know what you mean, it looks like most of the girls our age go to a different school. What else are you missing?'

'The canteen. Especially the pizzas, pastas and paninis - Italian is my favourite food group. The vending machines. The fact that the school was just down the road from where we lived. There were more pupils, I didn't feel weird about smoking and I could cadge the odd cig. I even miss some of the teachers; well, the female ones anyway.'

'I thought you liked Mr Brown.'

'He wasn't bad. Now when we do art that old woman comes in to teach it.'

'The teachers are older here.'

'And hairier.'

'And I can hardly understand what they're saying.'

'Haha. Do you remember when Mr Edison said "Look here" and I thought he wanted me to go and stand next to him?'

'The technology here is crap as well.'

'I can't understand why all the kids don't use a live connection for Xbox or PlayStations. They just go round to each other's houses when they want to play a game. It's weird.'

'And even though a lot of the kids have got mobiles, they hardly ever use them.'

'I know. They think it's pointless to text someone when they're sat in the same classroom.'

'At this rate, we'll end up listening to Mr Edison and learning something!'

'They don't think of mobiles as entertainment; they only use them in an emergency.'

'Exactly. And what kind of emergency is going to happen when they're just walking about the village? The biggest risk I've come across so far is from the sheep, which are nasty little sods.'

Chapter 48 – Operation Trash the Hash

Sunday was fairly uneventful in the shop and Luke was getting bored and restless. He was pretty uneasy about the plan and wasn't sure if James and Joey fully appreciated the consequences of messing around with the ABA. The only reassuring factor was that the ABA were no longer on their own turf and the fact that no one knew what kind of violence they had used in the past, meant that it might be easier to stand up to them. He considered that it had never occurred to any of them to contact the local police. Dealing with someone cheating in a race was one thing, but the likelihood of PC Barry or his colleagues being capable of tackling the ABA and stamping out a county lines operation was another. If a couple of the gang ever were arrested, they would quickly be replaced by someone more gullible and more enthusiastic.

According to Joey when PC Barry had been into the school in the past year and given a talk on drug use, it seemed to have the opposite effect. Luke liked PC Barry and felt oddly protective towards him but thought he might be better placed to tackle the gang himself, along with his friends. He also thought that he could deter more drug use with a few personal anecdotes of some of the people in his block of flats alone.

It was nearly time to close up and he was almost relieved that Tommo hadn't turned up. Just as he was putting some final items on the shelves for the following day, he smelt someone walk past him. The odour was so

247

pungent he recognised it as weed immediately. He followed the boy in the red hoody to the back of the shop where the perishable items were displayed for a quick sale. Luke quickly sent a message to the WhatsApp group that he had formed with James and Joey, called Operation Trash the Hash.

'Hes here.' He didn't have time for punctuation today.

Tommo, who was no big fan of the Atkins diet, grabbed a loaf, some crisps and a cake and headed to the till. Luke tried to engage him in conversation, but he was obviously not in a chatty mood. Luke then took as long as possible ringing up the items and pretending he didn't know how to enter the reduced prices until Tommo got narky. Unusually for a young person, Tommo paid with cash, shoved everything in his rucksack and headed out of the door.

As soon as they got his message Joey and James took arms full of the cannabis plants from inside as they decided they would be the quickest to burn. As James piled them into a bonfire and placed firelighters around them, Joey grabbed loads of the plants growing along the edge of the field. He didn't want to risk putting the fire out before it had got started so they both set fire to as many of the dry plants as possible and threw some lighter fuel over the bonfire. They gave it a couple of minutes to get established then piled the outside plants across the top.

The fumes were pretty pungent almost immediately and they both started laughing, never having experienced contact with any type of drugs before. Their nerves seemed to calm down a bit as they went on to the next stage of their operation. They grabbed hold of the struts at the back of the hut and pushed and pulled it into the field a bit. It was a struggle as it was heavy and their feet were getting bogged down in the mud. Eventually, they managed to pull the hut enough to block the view of the fire from the village, in the hope that Tommo and the villagers wouldn't arrive in time to save the plants.

Unfortunately, this allowed the wind to whip up the fire and very soon it was taller than they were, with flames rising high above them. They stood downwind and tried to sober up. 'We've been here ten minutes, we'd better get going,' said James. They hadn't done as much damage as they wanted to but couldn't risk staying any longer.

They ran partway down the hill, and as they climbed over the orange plastic security fencing into the building site they saw Tommo heading along the path. They were fairly sure he hadn't seen them. They quickly sent a text to Luke.

'Operation Trash the Hash pretty successful. C U later.'

Luke was really happy as he hopped on the bus to school. There had still not been any backlash from Tommo and the ABA so he was hoping they had all gone back to their own homes. He and Robbie sat on the back seat with Joey. Luke explained to Joey that their geography class would be going on a field trip to some mystery location, from where they would have to find their way back to school.

Robbie wanted to know if Joey knew where they would be dropped, but he told them that he had no idea. He did give them some tips such as remembering that the school had a couple of large hills behind it and a valley in front of it. The river ran down from the highest hill to the west of the building. There was a church in the town and the spire was often visible when other buildings were hidden by fog. The church was to the east of the school.

They tried to remember as much of the information as possible. They were split into two teams, with Luke and Robbie being put in charge of each. They would only be given an ordnance survey map, which they had been taught how to read in their geography lesson. The map covered an area of about ten square miles. The only place name was the school, which was shown as a small box. The hills were shown as a series of concentric circles that indicated how steep they were and the height above sea level. The railway line was indicated, as were the river and the main streams. There wasn't much other detail given.

After Robbie and Luke had been nominated as captains and had chosen their teams, Robbie couldn't resist saying to Luke, 'Don't worry; if you get lost, they will send out a search party for you! But try not to be too late; it's pasta for lunch today.'

Ralph, one of the boys in Luke's team whispered to his friend, 'We'd better make sure we're back first or there will be nothing left!'

The groups were driven in two separate mini-buses to different locations. They weren't far from each other, but they didn't know that. They couldn't see each other, as they were on opposite sides of a hill.

Luke tried to remember everything that Joey had said but couldn't recall whether the river ran down the west or east of the school. He was pretty sure that the rest of his group would have a good idea of where they were but didn't want to ask them unless he had to. He studied the map, but as it was just a series of lines, he found it difficult to work out. Then he remembered Joey saying that the river ran down the highest hill. The height of the hills was shown, so he could tell which was the highest one on the map, and he could see the river off to his left, therefore it had to be the one they were standing on now. The trouble was that from this vantage point, he couldn't tell if he should go forward or backwards.

The other boys were peering over his shoulder and desperate to give their advice. He was trying to make sure they could all see the map. Luke pointed to the hill that they were standing on the side of and said, 'How do we know if we are on this side of the hill or that? The compass will show us which way to go, but we need to know which way we are facing now.'

There were no visible buildings at all, and everywhere was just green hills covered in nothing more distinguishable than the odd flock of sheep. After several minutes of arguing amongst themselves, one of the boys pointed out the arrow at the top of the page that showed which way was north. If they were on the west of the hillside, the compass would show which way to go. Luke could have kicked himself for not observing such an obvious fact.

They set off down the hill and seemed to be making reasonable time. However, when they reached the bottom of the hill, they couldn't get across the river as it was far too wide and flowing too fast. 'Does anyone know where the nearest bridge is?' asked Luke.

None of them knew, so in the end, they decided to flip a coin to determine which way to go. They settled on going to the left, but after several minutes of walking, they had a discussion and thought it might be better to retrace their steps and go the other way. They walked on for about twenty more minutes and eventually found a footbridge. They crossed several fields and still there were no obvious landmarks.

Luke was beginning to worry about the mood of the group, particularly when Kieran said, 'I bet the other lot are back at school by now; we've wasted half an hour.'

'I doubt they will be. Robbie will be out of breath if he's had to travel anywhere near as much as we have, and he will be slowing his team down.'

'He might not be slowing them down if he knows which way to go. It might be easier from where they are.'

As they walked through the fields, it started to get a bit cooler and damper. There was a mist coming down in the distance, obscuring any possible landmarks. As the mist cleared a bit Ralph spotted the church spire in the distance. 'It's over there, we need to change direction. Then we've only got a couple more miles to school.'

They were all a lot more cheerful and ran for a few minutes until they came to a deep stream. Eventually, after a couple of minutes of searching, they found some stepping stones. On the opposite side, they saw a couple of thuggish-looking guys arguing with Tommo. They were cautious about approaching them, but they had no option. They went across in single file, slipping and panicking, trying to look down and avoid eye contact, then practically ran the rest of the way back to school. Luke had spotted Spud, Chucky and Tommo and rather than cross at the steppingstones, ducked behind a couple of the bigger lads and ran through the stream. He was soaked up to his calves and freezing, but he managed to avoid being seen.

They all hurried into the classroom and were thrilled to discover they were the first ones back. Ten minutes later Robbie's team made it back. His team were stunned when they saw that Luke's group had beaten them to it.

Mr Edison told them all to go and get lunch, and that they would discuss the trip afterwards.

The whole story soon emerged. It appeared that Robbie had used Scott's mobile to go onto the internet. As they had been high in the hills, he had had no trouble receiving a signal. He had requested details of the nearest café, and when three options came up, he selected the one near the school and asked for directions. They had simply followed the directions and, as Robbie had convinced them they would be sure to beat the other team, they popped into the café for a cup of hot chocolate. Then they sauntered over to the school to claim victory.

'But we were told to leave our phones with Mr Edison.' Said Ralph.

'I did leave mine. I borrowed Scott's.'

'Well, what went wrong?' Asked Luke incredulously.

'I d-d-don't know,' stammered Robbie. 'It brought us straight home; we didn't take any detours apart from the café, and we were only in there for a few minutes.'

As they were waiting for the bus home, Robbie asked Scott if he had any idea why it would have taken so long when they had such clear directions and hadn't diverted from them.

'Have you considered that the directions would probably follow the main paths and roads rather than travelling in a straight line through the fields?' Asked Scott.

Robbie looked like he could have kicked himself, and Scott.

The bus was a bit later than usual and Joey, Luke, Robbie and Scott were arguing about football as they jumped onto it. Luke had been a lifelong but indifferent supporter of Manchester United and for no obvious reason, Robbie had decided that he was now a Manchester City fan. They were trying to think up as many humiliating score lines and events as they could, to wind each other up.

Robbie said to Joey, 'don't mention Southampton, he gets really touchy.'

This roused Joey's curiosity. Luke didn't want to elaborate but Robbie told him of the occasion when United had played the Saints and at half time had changed their grey tops for blue. A decision they were fined for. Luke retaliated by telling him that Yaya Toure accidentally signed up for Manchester City instead of Manchester United because he thought there was only one club in Manchester! They settled down as they approached their stop.

The door of the little bus opened, and they were gathering their bags and coats when Spud and Chucky jumped on board. The driver, who was an ex-rugby player shouted at them, 'This is a school bus, you can't get on here,' only to be told to shut up. They covered the few paces to the back of the bus quickly and grabbed Robbie and Scott around their throats, lifting them off their seats. They were shouting obscenities and demanding to know if they had burnt their gear. As neither one of them had been involved in the operation they denied all knowledge.

Spud and Chucky turned their attention to Joey and Luke. Joey was in the middle seat on the back row so was the easiest to get to. He predicted Spud's move and cancelled it out by bringing his forearms together to stop the throat hold, grabbed Spud around the back of his neck and in one swift move pulled his head down and raised his knee. The crack of his nose breaking shocked them all.

Luke lifted his hands to protect his face from Chucky but took a couple of blows to the side of his head. He hadn't had many fights in his life but pushed his thumb into Chucky's eye. Chucky roared in pain and put his hand up to his eye. The driver unlocked his door and grabbed Chucky by the back of his hoody and spun him towards the front of the bus. He was about to take hold of Spud, but Spud snarled at him to get off. Spud left grudgingly, shouting threats and trailing blood along the aisle.

After Spud and Chucky stormed off the bus the driver locked the doors. He drove past the battle-grey BMW with blacked-out windows just as Spud and Chucky jumped in it. He accelerated away from the bus stop and along the narrow lane. The lads were checking behind them and shouting that they were being followed. As there were many twists and turns the driver had to keep slowing down, allowing the BMW to easily catch up with them. The driver shouted at the lads to stay in their seats and to stop looking over their shoulders as they were blocking his view. He was sure that they wouldn't keep up the pursuit and that they would soon get bored. But both Spud and Chucky had been involved in police pursuits in the past, as a result of their TWOCing (Taking WithOut Consent) careers and it was an unusual experience to be the ones doing the chasing.

The bus driver continued down into the village with the lads shouting suggestions as to how to outrun or outmanoeuvre the car, none of which were practical. Various villagers and pedestrians stopped and watched the pursuit, unsure of what was occurring. He drove on for a couple of miles and looped back around the other side of the hill and churned up loads of mud as he pulled up inside the building site in front of a huge concrete mixer, which hid them from view. There were some stunned faces from the various tradesmen on site and everyone on the bus held their breaths.

They couldn't see the BMW but they could see the trail of dust it kicked up as it went passed the site and carried on up the hill. The lads waited a couple of minutes and then jumped out of their seats. Before he would unlock the door the driver wanted to know what was going on. Robbie and Scott had no idea and Joey wanted to give the minimum amount of information; in case it got them into further trouble in the future. He said that the thugs were a couple of drug dealers who wanted to set up a county-lines operation, and they were refusing to cooperate. The driver took some convincing not to call the police but after accepting their explanation and thanks he opened the doors for them. The bus headed back to the depot and the

258

lads took a minute and headed towards Joey's house to regroup and gather their wits.

Once they were all seated in the living room, they all started talking at once. Joey asked them to stop and then gave them a brief history of recent events. He told Robbie and Scott about Tommo and the shepherd's hut; how he and James had failed to destroy the cannabis plants with vinegar; and then resorted to setting fire to the plants after Luke had let them know when the coast was clear.

Robbie and Scott had instantly recognised Spud and Chucky. They were filled with dread after their previous encounters back in Manchester.

It was now obvious that Tommo was part of a county-lines operation that was much bigger than they had realised.

They were all worried and decided they would need to go away and think of a way to try and rid the village of the drug dealers.

Chapter 51 - Social Evening

Robbie and Scott had decided they didn't want to be involved in any plans for retaliation regarding the cannabis plants and the ongoing county lines scheme, particularly since it was obvious that the ABA was somehow connected to it. The ABA hadn't left any graffiti in the village and Robbie probably wouldn't have felt inclined to deface it, even if they had. After his previous experience with Spud, he was too traumatised to risk any kind of reprisal. He had seriously considered seeking some kind of help but hadn't felt strong enough to talk about the event, not even to his mum or Luke.

Joey, James and Luke had been discussing various options and had decided that there was only one solution, and it would need to be pulled off as soon as possible when Luke wasn't working in the shop. Unfortunately, he had agreed to work all day Saturday so it would need to be sometime on Sunday.

Luke was trying to act normally on Saturday and went to work as usual with his mum. Catherine asked him to put two posters in the shop window. One was advertising for additional tradesmen for the building site, and one was advertising the next dance at the village hall. It sounded boring but he listened as she told him and Beth that there were regular events held there, including monthly dances, mums and tots group, chess club, and fairs held at Easter, Christmas and summer. The dances were the most popular events, with young people coming from several of the outlying villages and farms. There was always a big bonfire on the fifth of November in a nearby field, and Paul and William helped out with fireworks; Catherine and several of the other ladies organised food and games such as apple bobbing.

'The dance is great fun and always well attended. You would probably like it as well as Robbie,' suggested Catherine.

He didn't think that was very likely.

Beth asked Catherine what kind of music they played and was told it was an eclectic mix of chart music, jazz and rock and roll. Whenever possible there was a live band. This month it was a Michael Bublé tribute act.

'I bet your Nan would enjoy it.' Beth said to Luke.

'Yes, probably. But I'm not going.'

Luke's Nan liked all types of music and particularly enjoyed singing songs from musicals. He was surprised that he hadn't had much time to think about her recently and they hadn't seen her since they had moved to the village. He suddenly felt a bit sad and realised he missed having her to talk to.

Catherine explained that everyone attended, including young people. It allowed them to meet their friends, and they weren't put off by the older music; they just came along and had fun.

'I doubt me and Robbie will.'

Luke and Beth had occasionally eaten an evening meal in the farmhouse, cooked by William. That evening after dinner, Beth mentioned the dance and asked William if he had ever been to one of them. He told her that it was something he enjoyed and attended often. He mentioned that Fred from the farm next door had been to the last couple and spent the evening mooning over Catherine. He didn't have the nerve to ask her to dance or even to buy her a drink.

Beth said that for Catherine's sake, it was hoped his courage never developed enough to allow him to.

William mentioned that James and Joey always attended. That piqued Luke's curiosity as he couldn't imagine them going to something that he thought was really for old people.

'Well, they play all kinds of music; it's not just old-fashioned music all evening. The youngsters don't dance much, well apart from some of the girls; they just stand around chatting. Some of the kids from the remote farms don't get to socialise much, so it's a good opportunity for them.'

'Well, when do they have things for people my age?'

'They have a monthly disco, where they play whatever the kids want.'

Beth asked if the people working on the building site came.

'Well, they've only been working here for a couple of months; maybe they will come when they see how popular it is. And it's not as if there are loads of other things going on in the evening, is it? Paul sometimes comes along, and Catherine with her mum, Sally.'

'Well, I thought about asking my mum; she loves all types of music, especially from musicals.'

'Well, you should invite her then,' said William.

'The problem is I don't think she would be able to get back home the same evening. She'll have to get two buses and a train. Would you have any objection if she stayed in the caravan overnight?'

'Of course not. But if there's not enough room she could always stay in my spare room. You could make the spare bed up for her. And as you say, if she likes all types of music, she would probably enjoy it. Has she been to the village yet?'

'She came with me before Damian got the job, just so that we could see what the area was like. She thought it was peaceful and pretty.'

'Well, perhaps she would like to stay for the weekend. You could show her around. Luke could show her Capel Garmon and the fountains; that is if she's steady on her feet.'

Luke said that his nan was usually pretty steady on her feet and thought it best not to mention what she was like when she had drunk a few of her favourite martini cocktails.

'She'll probably be fine staying in the caravan. But I will ask if she would like to stay for the weekend, as long as she can get the time off work,' said Beth.

'Where does she work?' asked William.

'At The Printworks,' replied Beth.

The Printworks was a complex that housed several restaurants, bars, clubs and a cinema. It was originally a

Victorian printing company. But as modern printing techniques changed, they didn't need such huge rooms for the production and printing of newspapers, so it had been converted to its current status a few years earlier. The entrance still had the old cobbles, and the building was made of old red brick. However many of the windows had been blacked out and the walls were now painted in dark colours to give them a permanent night-time atmosphere. Jan worked in one of the bars. Unfortunately, William imagined her working as a secretary or administrator, helping to produce a newspaper or some such.

'Surely she doesn't have to work over the weekend?' asked William.

'Yes, she does. It's open seven days a week, but she only works for five days.'

That made sense to William. After all, newspapers are printed every day of the week.

Perhaps because she was a grandmother, he assumed she was elderly, but like her daughter she had given birth when she was only fifteen, making her exactly forty-six.

Chapter 52 – Operation Hide the Hut

The following morning Joey and James woke up early and packed some sandwiches and water into a small rucksack. They made sure their mobiles were fully charged and they wore warm clothes. As they had to cover quite a bit of ground they were taking their bikes and took the precaution of letting down the front tyre on their dad's bike, in case he suggested going out with them.

They were going to borrow their dad's site keys but realised that his front door key was on the same keyring. The large Yale key looked the most likely one for the gate and James was trying to remove it when they heard Paul coming downstairs. He stuffed them in his pocket and asked his dad if he wanted a cup of tea. Paul said yes and asked what they were up to. They looked guiltily at one another, and both started babbling at the same time. He asked them to slow down.

'We're going for a bike ride,' said James.

'If you hang on for a minute, I'll come with you,' said Paul.

'Dad, it looks like you've got a puncture. Never mind. If you're staying home, can you wash my uniform?' Asked Joey.

'Oh, great, thanks for that. Don't worry about me, slaving away.'

'Actually, I've got some washing too,' said James as he ran upstairs. He then quickly removed the key and when he returned to the kitchen with some laundry, dropped the rest in the bowl.

'See you later Dad,' they shouted together.

'That was close, have you got the key?' Asked Joey.

'Yes, have you heard from Luke? Asked James.

'Yes, he's waiting at the edge of the site, behind a hedge.'

They jumped on their bikes and quickly headed over to where Luke was waiting for them. They were both jittery as they hid their bikes behind one of the old stone walls and walked to the site entrance with Luke.

'Are you certain no one will be working today?' Asked Luke.

'My dad said they never work Sundays as they have to pay double rates,' said James.

The three of them went to the gate, and as James tried the key in the lock, Joey and Luke were peering over his shoulder. He asked them to stand back as they were making him even more nervous and eventually he managed to open the padlock. They walked into the site and James pulled the gates closed and carefully looped the chain back around them so that they would look secure to a casual passer-by. Going over to the south side of the site, taking care not to fall into any open footings, they found an area behind a partially constructed garage and watched the shepherd's hut for movement. The weather was a bit cold and once their initial nerves had calmed down they were complaining of boredom.

Luke checked his pocket for the tenth time for the key to the tractor, which he knew was William's pride and joy.

'I should go and check that the tractor is still in the middle field,' said Luke.

'What if it isn't? What if William has moved it up to the farmyard?' Asked Joey anxiously.

'You'll have to go and distract him and put the radio on or something so he can't hear me start it up.'

'Well go and find out where it is, then we'll have to decide what to do. If it's in one of the lower fields you might be spotted driving it over to the hut,' said James.

'If it is there, I'll stay with it and whistle to let you know.'

Staying low, Luke ran off to the middle field. His heart sank when he saw the field standing empty. He ran the length of the field and crossed the stream. He constantly scanned all around and eventually saw the edge of the bright yellow vehicle in the field nearest to the farmhouse. Knowing that he may not get a 'phone signal he ran back to the others and said that he would need Joey to get rid of William for a while.

Joey ran up to the farmhouse and knocked on the door. When William answered he said that his dad was having a problem changing his tyre and needed some help. William assumed it was his car tyre so went to find his torque wrench and jack. As William set off across the yard Joey said that he was going to call for Luke and would see him later. As soon as he was out of sight he ran over to the tractor and jumped into the passenger seat as Luke climbed up into the driver's seat.

Luke had recently acquired the spare key and put it in the ignition and after several false starts, it eventually started up. It had been parked in a corner and had to be reversed out, a manoeuvre he had never carried out. He was nervous and distracted as Joey was suggesting various buttons and levers to press. He finally found reverse gear but when he turned the wheel right the tractor went left. It was getting closer to the wall and in danger of crashing into it. With Joey's constant instructions he was getting stressed, so he had to ask him to stop talking.

'Okay, but I think you need to turn the wheel left if you want it to go right.' Said Joey.

'I've worked that out for myself!' He snapped.

He moved back enough so that he could drive through the gate and down the lane, praying that no one would approach from the opposite direction. They passed a couple of hillwalkers who pressed up against the hedgerow to avoid being run over. When they could see the northern edge of the site, they pulled off the road and were perilously close to falling into a ditch.

Joey was shouting and swearing, and Luke told him to shut up again. James could hear the approaching tractor so ran to meet them.

'You need to keep it down, if Tommo comes out of his hut, he might hear you.'

Joey and Luke jumped out of the tractor and ran back to the original lookout post. They had to wait over half an hour for Tommo to finally show himself. From monitoring his movements over the past few weeks, they had concluded that he had very few habits, but he always went home early on Sunday mornings, with a sports bag of presumably dirty laundry. James and Luke had only noticed this because they had been training for the race before Luke went to work in the shop. Tommo's home life was pretty chaotic. His mother had not been able to work following a tragic incident several years before and had become reliant on alcohol to get her through the awful days. Most of the villagers felt sorry for both of them.

They waited until he was some distance away before the three of them jumped on the tractor, with James hanging off the edge of Joey's seat. The field was very uneven and they bounced around a lot. Only Luke found it funny.

As they approached the edge of the building site, James jumped down, locked the gates and pocketed the key. He ran the rest of the way to the hut through the unused field, arriving just after Luke and Joey on the tractor. As Luke reversed the tractor so that he could go straight up the hill to William's farm, James and Joey made sure there were no naked flames or anything dangerous in the hut. They threw out Tommo's old trainers and bedding as well as a small heater but kept the hundreds of little cannabis plants.

Turning the hut around in the muddy field was harder than they expected, and they were all covered in mud before they finally connected it to the tow bar on the tractor. Eventually, the three of them jumped aboard the tractor and Luke drove it again. He thought he was quite a good driver, but his passengers clearly didn't agree. Hoping that William hadn't yet returned, they went to the far barn and dropped the hut off. As James and Joey pushed it to the back of the barn and put bales of hay all around it, Luke prepared to return the tractor.

As he was approaching the edge of the farmhouse, he saw William coming up the lane. Jumping down from the cab he started to say he wanted to show James and Joey that he could drive, but William was in no mood to listen. Seeing James and Joey coming over he shouted, 'That tractor is a very expensive piece of equipment and is not for showing off on.' Luke apologised and asked if there was any work he needed doing.

'Yes, actually, the sheep need dagging.'

'Is that removing the matted wool from the sheep's backside?'

'It is, and it'll take the three of you most of the day. I'll put the kettle on.'

Chapter 53 – The Red Dress

It was the day of the dance and Luke was working in the shop. He was bored to tears listening to his mum and Catherine discussing what they were going to wear. Beth had bought a new red dress that was quite fitted and just down to her knees. She had bought some red sandals as well and was going to paint her nails and get her hair done. Catherine was going to wear a plain black dress which Luke thought she would look anything but plain in. They were in a gossiping mood and took it in turns guessing what Sandra would wear. Beth thought she would buy a new outfit, especially for the occasion – it would probably be a tracksuit – in purple. Catherine thought she might surprise them all and wear something thigh-skimming with lots of cleavage on show.

'I don't think that's likely,' said Beth.

'Well, you said she dresses inappropriately.'

'That's true. Perhaps she'll just have her usual botox and lip fillers so she can spend the evening pouting and posting pictures of herself.'

Beth asked Catherine if her mum and Genevieve would be coming, and she mumbled something about them not being able to, then quickly moved the conversation on.

Catherine asked Luke if he intended to come to the dance, but he had been overwhelmingly unenthusiastic at the prospect. If he did decide to go, he hoped Tommo and the ABA wouldn't turn up, as he was still scared of future retribution.

Catherine pointed out that there would be plenty to eat and drink, that lots of young people attended from the area and that she had been informed by Lloyd Morgan's mum that the whole family would be going. He didn't seem too keen to meet Lloyd again, but when she mentioned that he had a younger sister who was extremely attractive, he warmed slightly to the idea.

'I've never seen her at school,' said Luke.

'You wouldn't have. She goes to an all-girls school, miles away.'

'There don't seem to be many girls my age at school,'

'That's because the girls' school has a great reputation.'

'I'll mention it to James and Joey to see if they're going,' he said.

Luke thought if he spoke to James and Joey, they might be able to help him convince Robbie and Scott to go too. There was more safety in numbers, as reluctant as Robbie and Scott were to get involved in anything to do with the ABA.

After work, as Beth was getting ready, Luke had agreed to go to the bus stop to meet his Nan. He decided to jog to the bus stop as he had been training for the Manchester Half Marathon. As she jumped from the bus, he took her overnight bag and kissed her on the cheek.

'Hi Nan, we've missed you.'

'Thanks, love' she said, genuinely touched.

'It's alright,' Luke replied.

'William owns the farm that you live at now, doesn't he? What's he like?' She queried.

272

'He's great. He's taught me all kinds of things including how to get the soil ready for crops, when to plant stuff, and when to pick it. He's even taught me drystone walling, and I'm going to enter a competition where you get so many hours and bricks, and you have to build a section of wall.'

Jan could hardly believe that this was her grandson speaking. She had little knowledge or experience of drystone walling and the like but was pleasantly surprised to hear Luke talk knowledgeably on the subject.

He showed her where the running route was for the race he had recently run and mentioned that he sometimes ran to school as part of his training for the Manchester half-marathon.

When they arrived at the farmhouse, after what felt like a long trek to Jan, they were met by a wonderful smell of home cooking. William was making a huge pan of chicken soup and had baked some fresh bread. They all ate some before they left, as the food wouldn't be served until later in the evening. There was a nice, friendly atmosphere with them all chatting together. Luke's nan always knew how to break down barriers and make people feel relaxed.

Then they strolled down to the village hall. There were lots of people milling about, inside and out, chatting and laughing. The atmosphere was friendly and warm, and Luke was glad he came.

Over to the right of the doors, there were several people whom Luke didn't recognise, but amongst them were Huw and Frances Morgan. Standing nearby was their son

Lloyd and a gorgeous blonde girl in a lovely red dress, who was Lloyd's sister Hayley. He spotted James and Joey and walked over to join them.

'So, you've noticed Lloyd's here then,' said Joey.

'I don't think it was Lloyd he was staring at,' said James.

'Well, who else does he know from Llugwy?' Asked Joey.

'Nobody you fool. But Lloyd's brought his sister Hayley along,' stated James.

'He always brings her; what's the big deal?' Asked Joey innocently.

James and Luke exchanged a glance but didn't say anything more.

Shortly afterwards they were joined by Robbie and Scott. Robbie immediately asked, 'have you seen that girl in the red dress? Who is she? Does she live around here?'

Several of the younger people had downloaded playlists and a few of these were played first. Nobody danced; they just stood around the edges of the dance floor chatting and laughing. At about nine the food was served and everyone tried to find a seat to perch on. Some old standards were played whilst everyone was eating.

The tribute band tuned up their instruments and then played a few Michael Bublé numbers to encourage some dancing. Several of the older people filed onto the dance floor. Luke overhead his Nan ask William if he would accompany her. As Catherine was collecting some of the plates, his mum looked a bit lonely, and he felt sorry for her.   Sandra was with Andrew and chatting away animatedly.

As Luke was glancing over at Hayley in what he considered to be a surreptitious manner, Paul came over and asked Beth if she'd like a drink. She said she'd love one and followed him over to the bar. They finished their drinks and as the music changed to a mellow number, they started dancing close together. Paul was holding Beth quite closely and as the music finished, he bent down and kissed her on the lips. Luke and James were mortified but both managed to appear commendably nonchalant.

As the evening wore on, the room was pretty packed – everyone who had been milling about outside was now inside, soaking up the atmosphere and alcohol as well as any remaining food. Robbie was doing his bit for the environment by reducing the amount of leftovers going to landfill.

Luke was convinced that Hayley had smiled, albeit tentatively, at him. James was sure that she was looking over at him. Scott and Joey, who had been running in and out all evening, complained they hadn't got a drink. In the absence of Robbie, Luke assumed responsibility for getting a drink for Scott and agreed to go to the bar. James decided that he would also need to go to the bar to get one for Joey. The journey to the bar involved a convoluted trip around the perimeter of the room, which necessitated them walking past Hayley.   As they approached her group they couldn't see her, although they had both glimpsed her red dress only moments before. Luke then thought he saw her ahead of him and pushed through the people standing around the bar, intending to ask if she would like a drink. As she turned around, he was horrified to recognise his mum.

'Hello love are you having a nice time?' she asked him.

'Err, yes, it's fine. I'm just getting a drink,' he replied.

'I haven't seen your Nan for a while. The last time I saw her she was dancing with William. I don't know where they get the energy,' she stated.

Luke was far too embarrassed to contemplate how much energy William and his nan might have. Paul offered to get him a drink, but he declined, feeling that he would seem a bit childish, and moved along the bar to get served. James was immediately behind him and told his dad that he would get drinks for himself and Joey. Paul and Beth decided to take their drinks outside where it was a little bit cooler and quieter.

There was a fair amount of jostling at the bar and Luke felt someone push in near his left side. He glanced across cautiously in case it was Lloyd and saw the red dress. He was about to say something to his mum when he realised it was Hayley. Just then the barman approached him and asked if he was next.

'No, I don't think so. I think it's her next,' he said gallantly.

She smiled at him archly, ordered her drink, then turned on her heel and walked away. She didn't even thank him and he could have kicked himself for not offering to buy her a drink. He wasn't bothered, he told himself. James saw the exchange and was secretly pleased that Luke hadn't started chatting to her.

As the evening wore on, people started to drift off. Luke thought he saw Hayley glancing in his direction, and she appeared to be getting ready to leave with her friends. He was desperately trying to think of something to say to her as she passed him and quickly dismissed, 'Would you like to dance?', 'Can I have your number?', 'Would you like a drink?', particularly since the bar was now closed. What he said was, 'When I saw you in that dress, I thought you were my mum.'

Oh God, he thought, had he really said that? She walked past him wordlessly. He got some strange looks from her friends as they walked out. He was relieved James didn't appear to have heard him. However, Robbie had finished Hoovering up the leftovers and was right behind him.

'What do you mean? She doesn't look much like your mum to me.'

Luke had been desperate to take part in the half-marathon in Manchester for so long, he could hardly believe the day had finally arrived. He wished Mr Strachan could see him now and hoped he would be proud of him.

He was looking forward to showing James and Joey his hometown. He thought they would be impressed, particularly since the route would take in some of the most famous and iconic buildings in Manchester. Of course, Joey would still be too young to participate but had decided to come along for the ride with his dad and they planned to stand near the finishing line to cheer on Luke, James, Rhodri and Gavin. Luke would have liked his mum to come too but she had to work and was a bit uneasy about the risk of bumping into Damian. Luke wasn't bothered if he did bump into him. He no longer felt any need to be civil to him for his mum's sake and he didn't sense any risk in returning to Manchester, certain that the ABA wouldn't be interested in the marathon.

As they approached the outskirts of Manchester, Luke pointed out some of the landmarks such as his old school which seemed impressive to James and Joey.

'Didn't you get lost in it?' Asked Joey.

'I did during my first year, but I soon found my way around. You have to learn quickly in a place like that.'

'What do you mean?'

'Well, I went through the wrong door once and couldn't get back in so I had to walk around the back of the gym. That was when I discovered all the smokers and worse. I never made that mistake again.'

They had set off early, with Paul driving. As well as their car, there was a car full of the builders. Only Rhodri and Gavin were going to run, but two of the other men who were originally from Manchester would watch the race and then meet up with a couple of old friends for a drink. As some of the race was to be televised live Catherine intended to live stream it now that the internet café was up and running. She didn't think there would be much chance of being able to spot Luke, James or the others amongst the thousands of other runners, even though they were wearing t-shirts with the Welsh dragon emblazoned across the front.

Several members of the media were present, all holding huge microphones with their logos displayed on them. Amongst them were representatives from the BBC, Radio Lancashire, Capital FM and Granada Reports. As they joined the queue to register, they were approached by a member of the Granada Reports team.

'Good morning, I'm Ranjita Singh with Granada Reports, the local television station, I'm just doing a few live interviews for this morning's news programme. Can I ask you a couple of questions please?'

'Yes of course,' replied Gavin on behalf of them all.

'Can I ask which charity you're running on behalf of?'

'We are all running for Cerebral Palsy as Luke has a school friend who has the condition and will hopefully take part himself in future years.'

'That's admirable. I'm sure they'll appreciate the support. Can I ask why you're all wearing the dragon t-shirts?'

'Well most of us are from Wales, but Luke here is a local lad.'

'Hello, Luke, and which area are you from?'

'I'm from Ardwick, but I recently moved to Rowan.'

'And which school did you go to?'

Luke told her and she asked if he wanted to say hello to any of his old school friends.

'Well, I would like to say hello to two of my old teachers, Mr Strachan and Miss Littleton.'

'I'm sure they'll be proud of you. We wish you the best of luck.'

They moved along the queue and went through the registration process. Luke tucked the microchip into his shoe. This would record all the stations he passed through and calculate his time at the end of the race. He would be able to put his details on the website after the event and see his position in the runners and his exact time. He didn't expect to be in the fastest group, but he did think he would be able to complete it in a reasonable time as it was on a flat surface, which was a lot easier than the hills and valleys of Rowan.

The professional runners were to set off before everyone else and Luke, James, Gavin and Rhodri were near the front of the second group. They had decided that they would try and stick together as it would be easier to find everyone at the end of the race. As they set off they ran under a huge banner that said: "Good luck, see you at the finish".

They started at Oxford Road, past the train station, and Deansgate locks then past the Hilton Hotel. They experienced 'Bands on the Run' when they ran through an area where the speakers were playing pumping music which made them all lengthen their strides, then just as they started to tire again, they passed Old Trafford. The crowds were huge and they cheered and clapped everyone as they passed. Luke nearly tripped as he thought he saw Spud's head in the distance. He kept scanning the crowd but couldn't see him again. They were all feeling the pain in their shins and whenever there was a drinks station they all slowed down to grab a much-welcome bottle of water. Soon they were looping past the Lowry with its distinctive building in the shape of a ship.

Luke was finally able to appreciate running through Manchester without any traffic to contend with. He was soaking up the atmosphere of the crowds constantly cheering and clapping. The next place of note on the route was the Imperial War Museum of the North - a striking building, clad in aluminium, it represented the world shattered by war. Just as they were passing through the 'runner's shower' Luke was grabbed and pulled to one side.

'What the?' He stuttered.

'Just listen, Luke. Spud saw you on television half an hour ago. He's trying to get some of the ABA together and they're going to get you before the end of the race,' said Natasha.

'Shit, where are they waiting?'

'I don't know, it could be anywhere towards the end of the route.'

'Thanks, I'll keep my eyes open.'

The brief exchange had meant that he had lost his group of friends and he was trying to see past a giant Darth Vader and several other Star Wars characters. He suddenly felt vulnerable and nervous. He couldn't believe his bad luck. He wanted to be stoic and just try and ignore them, after all, what could they do in front of all these witnesses? Then he remembered the next part of the race would take him through Trafford Ecological Park which was a local nature reserve giving sanctuary to wildlife such as newts and kestrels. Luke didn't think there would be much sanctuary for him. He decided that he would be much safer with the others and tried to find the energy to speed up and rejoin them. He tried to dodge to the left of Darth Vader but there wasn't enough space, so he tried to get between him and Princess Leia. She shouted at him for bumping into her and in the end, he decided he was less afraid of her than he was of being left isolated with the ABA so he barged past her. She lost her footing slightly and bumped into Chewbacca who fell over, taking several Jedi Knights with him. They swore angrily at Luke as he ran past them and he responded with 'Let the force be with you,' and put his fingers up in what he thought was supposed to be the sign of peace. They responded in like fashion and Darth Vader tried to hit him with his lightsabre.

Luke forced himself to sprint to catch up with the others. He passed a couple of people running for Cancer Research, then a huge bloke in a pink tutu with two nuns. One was exceptionally small and one was exceptionally tall but they both had pinched red faces under their habits. As he ran he thought there was an equal chance of his lungs bursting or his legs collapsing under him.

He could see the others just ahead and they turned to see where he was. They slowed down to give him time to catch up and James asked him if he was okay.

'Well, I've just met a girl I used to know.'

'Aye aye, this is not the time for romance boyo,' said Rhodri.

'She told me that her boyfriend is waiting for me.'

'Boyfriend? Oh, bad luck.'

'Yes and he's with a gang. I think I should just pull out and go and find Joey and Paul.'

'No way. You're not pulling out. You've trained hard for this.'

'I know but there could be a few of them.'

'Well there's a few of us, and we're Welsh.'

'What difference does that make?'

'We fight dirty.'

'They fight dirty.'

'They won't want to fight men.'

'That won't bother them, they'll have weapons.'

'Well, we'll have to improvise. There's a water station ahead, grab two bottles each lads.'

They didn't have enough breath to form a clear plan, but they decided that Luke should be in front as none of the others would recognise the gang. They had agreed on the signal that Luke would give if he saw them. As they entered the park Luke felt more and more uneasy. He was constantly scanning the area for Spud and the rest of the ABA.

There were quite a few late spring flowers in bloom, as well as a beautiful yellow forsythia bush. But Luke didn't register how lovely the area was, he was suspicious of every single person. There were fewer spectators in the park, they were mostly old people out for a Sunday morning stroll or couples with young kids. As they ran past the boating lake with its ancient weeping willows trailing in the water Luke thought he saw something, but it turned out to be a park attendant angrily scraping up some dog mess with his shovel and throwing it into his cart. Unfortunately, this act caught Luke's attention and he barely had time to register Spud and Chucky right ahead of him. He quickly raised his left hand so that the rest of the group would know the gang were on his left and was relieved when he realised there were only two of them, then raised his right when he realised the gang were actually on both sides of the path. 'Shit,' he thought, 'there're at least six of them.'

Spud lunged at Luke, swinging his fist high. Using a technique he'd learned from William with the sheep, Luke used Spud's momentum and grabbed his raised arm and swung him into Chucky and Travis. Chucky fell backwards but Travis merely sidestepped and hit Luke

284

cleanly on the chin with a solid knuckleduster. Luke's head was spinning, and it was as much as he could do to stay upright. Fish and Jordy saw their chance and were about to attack Luke when Rhodri and Gavin grabbed one each. Rhodri grabbed the collar of Fish's jacket, swung him around and gave him a swift punch in the kidneys. Gavin punched Jordy in the belly, knocking all the wind out of him, and he literally slithered to the floor and stayed there. A few runners sidestepped the melee and kept on running, not wanting to be drawn into any unpleasantness.

Spud recovered his footing and came back at Luke. As Spud raised his leg to kick Luke, James tested his memory of Tae Kwon do and delivered a roundhouse kick that sent Spud into an unfortunate backward sprawl that saw him landing on top of the gardener's cart.

'Argh,' he bellowed as he used his hands to lever himself out of the cart and the dog mess slithered in between his fingers.

Rhodri and Gavin tipped the contents of their bottles all over him.

'There you go boyo. That should cool you down a bit.'

At this point, the rest of the gang gathered their mediocre wits and ran away across the park in the direction of the main road.

For some ridiculous reason, Spud stood his ground and seriously considered continuing the fight. Everyone stood frozen, wondering what action he was going to take next. He shouted some obscenities and turned and walked away with as much dignity as someone covered in such a foul-smelling mess could do.

When he had put some distance between them he shouted, 'this isn't over.'

They all laughed awkwardly for a few minutes then Gavin took charge.

'He's right lads. We've got a race to finish.'

'I'm not sure I want to now,' replied Luke, who was feeling utterly defeated by this event.

'We're nearly at the finish line. It's only another mile or so. Come on,' said Rhodri.

'I don't think I can, my head is throbbing. You lot carry on and I'll go and find Joey and Paul.'

'No! We started this race together and we're going to finish it together. Pour a bit of that water over you, it'll clear your head.'

Noticing the Star Wars weirdoes entering the park finally settled it for Luke. He tipped the water over his head and face, threw the bottle in the rubbish cart and started to run. The others were a bit surprised at his sudden enthusiasm but dropping their bottles in the cart, they ran after him.

The last part of the race took them along Chester Road which became Deansgate and listening to everyone clapping them as they passed the finish line almost made Luke forget his aching head. The four of them formed a straight line and passed under the finish post together. They didn't break any records, not even personal records, but they felt like they'd achieved something good together.

They collected their belongings from the lockers and set about finding Paul and Joey. Joey had sent a text to say they were standing near Beetham Tower which contained the famous Cloud 23 Skybar, just a short walk away. They strolled over to meet them. Luke tried to keep his face turned away but they couldn't help but notice the huge swelling lump on his chin.

'What happened to you? Did you fall over?' Asked Joey.

'Joey, we've just finished a long race. We're knackered. Leave him alone,' said James.

'I was only asking. He falls over all the time when he's running at home,' muttered Joey.

'You fall over all the time when you're running at home,' replied James.

'Well, it's slippery there. This is a flat road.'

'Just drop it.'

Paul informed them that he had booked a table at a pub slightly out of the city centre as he thought it would be easier to get served and he had parked in the car park. As they took them in the direction of the pub, Luke asked the name of it.

'The Old Crow.'

Author note:

This is a complete work of fiction, however, the names of roads and districts in Manchester are real. The Manchester half-marathon route has changed over the years, so it may differ from the route I have used. The schools in Ardwick and Llugwy are entirely fictional and any resemblance to actual schools or teachers is coincidental. The village of Rowan is also fabricated, although there is a similarly named village, Rowen, in north Wales.

Printed in Great Britain
by Amazon

23551223R00161